Cinico

Travels with a Good Professor
at the Time of the Scottish Referendum

Allan Cameron

In which a narrator pretends to be the author and a perverse author pretends to be a translator who in his ensuing confusion drinks himself to death, causing a dispute between the fictional editor, the fictional author, his fictional wife and the translator's fictional widow, solely to illustrate the enlightened and enlightening chaos of translation, when the true purpose of this novel is to present conflicting views on nation, nationalism, power, class and the Scottish referendum.

Vagabond Voices
Glasgow

Published on 18 September 2017 by
Vagabond Voices Publishing Ltd.,
Glasgow,
Scotland.

ISBN 978-1-908251-82-4

Printed and bound in Poland

Cover design by Mark Mechan

Typeset by Park Productions

The publisher acknowledges subsidy towards
this publication from Creative Scotland

ALBA | CHRUTHACHAIL

The author acknowledges the assistance
of the FABER residency in Catalonia to
the writing of this novel

For further information on Vagabond Voices, see the website,
www.vagabondvoices.co.uk

For Margaret, Bertie, May Jo and the two Montanari families who introduced me to the pleasant town of Lugo di Romagna some forty-five years ago and more recently provided me with anecdotes useful to the writing of this novel

Contents

My Travels with a Good Professor

by

Cinico de Oblivii

Translated from the Italian
by Allan Cameron

Editor's Preface

When Allan Cameron first came to my office with his translation of Cinico de Oblivii's experience of the Scottish referendum, I could hardly have guessed at the problematic ramifications of this text. He was in a bullish mood, partly because he really cared about this book, as only a translator can, but I also suspected him of having taken a liquid lunch that made him even more expansive and exaggerated in his claims.

I agreed with him, however, that a non-fiction work that examined the whole phenomenon through the eyes of a foreign journalist – from the outside, as it were – would give an alternative perspective to the well-rehearsed arguments we remember from those times, and promised to read his English version. It was not easy to get him to leave, and for some time the manuscript lay in the pile on the floor next to my desk.

De Oblivii never found an Italian publisher for his original work. I don't know how hard he tried, and now I have been in touch with him, I sense that he probably didn't make much of an effort. It's also true that this book is in many ways more of interest to us than it would be to the reading public in Italy.

My principal purpose for writing this preface to what is after all a non-fiction work is that I wish to warn the reader of some of its limitations. The text is eccentric, to say the least, having gone through various metamorphoses. Cinico de Oblivii, who worked for one of the lesser-known Italian newspapers, kept notes of the various meetings he had whilst reporting on the Scottish referendum. Many of those meetings appear to have been recorded for their colour and not their relevance, and his own vicissitudes and musings are not excluded either. Those conversations were obviously in English, but he wrote them down in Italian, and then our translator Allan Cameron – sadly no longer with us – translated them back into English. Cameron was an erratic worker and occasionally less than meticulous. He was not above putting his own spin on things – "embellishments" he called them. So not only eccentric, but also likely to be unreliable.

Nevertheless, I decided that this is a curious and even instructive work worthy of being published for the benefit of those interested in such an important event in our national history, even though I am not personally sympathetic to De Oblivii's Damascene conversion to the cause of Scottish independence, which I suspect was determined more by his sentimental liaisons than by any rational analysis of an extremely complex subject.

I am personally acquainted with George Lovenight, the "good professor" he so cruelly denigrates, and his victim has graciously raised no objection to the publication, which he believes will be read only by those in the media and academe interested in gaining the fullest picture of the referendum, who will see through the obvious fallacies in the author's thinking.

The matter was further complicated when, after we'd completed the editorial stage, Allan Cameron tragically died on a beach in Lewis at the foot of some concrete steps, having fallen asleep as the tide was coming in. His widow argued that he had written the whole thing himself and that this is an entirely fictional work.

Of course the matter had to be investigated, and fortunately we were able to locate De Oblivii's ex-wife and through her to contact the author himself, who now lives in Greece. We thought then that the matter was resolved, but the author, who is as laid-back as Cameron was excitable, said that although he was indeed the author of this work, he was not interested in the rights – even the moral right to be acknowledged as the author. He said that he liked Cameron's translation and wouldn't change a word of it. He wouldn't be drawn on whether or not some of the commentary was invented by Cameron, a notorious supporter of the Yes campaign. But having spoken to him several times on the phone and having eventually received a letter from him, I believe that De Oblivii is quite capable of producing the one-sided observations we encounter herein.

Initially his estranged wife was insisting that he should not give up the rights. Her behaviour was difficult to understand, given the nature of the book, but she relented in her second letter (these letters are published at the end of the book). Until she came round to our position, it looked as though *Cinico* would not be published, but this family appears to have put aside its disagreements and made a decision. All rights including those of authorship would pass to the deceased translator and therefore to his heirs. De Oblivii would be acknowledged on what is usually called the half-title page. We allowed De Oblivii to restore some of the comments we had found contentious and disputed with Cameron. It was a messy deal, but it's one that has more or less satisfied all parties and has allowed this small project to go ahead – this little piece to be added to the jigsaw.

I am half Italian and have some command of the language, though far from fluent. For this reason, I became personally involved in the editing. Most of the notes were provided by Cameron, and where their provenance is not mentioned, they belong to him. The few that I provided are distinguished by the wording, "editor's note".

Robert Remescioni, Vagabond Voices

I

The Author Grows Up, Has a Family and Finds a Job in London All within One Brief Chapter

I came into this world to observe and not to understand, to record and not to persuade. So it is with humility that I approach this task, but that humility may be false. In every small man, as I now realise myself to be – though not without a little pride and relief at my smallness – there is a megalomaniac. Do not be afraid, because this isn't the story of a megalomaniac who wanted to get out and rule the world; this was a megalomaniac who was very much in his place: a megalomaniac who wandered around, and looked, listened and wrote down, a megalomaniac who dreamt and derived his self-importance from being above and beyond all things, like the powerless, omniscient narrator of a traditional novel. This was a megalomaniac who thought that he had sorted it all out, except for a few tiny gaps in his knowledge that awaited degustation like exotic sweetmeats – tasty but irrelevant and unnecessary to the business of life. And what is more, my megalomania stretched to the absolute obligation and craving to persuade my fellow London hacks at the Pig and Whistle, Cafemania and Drop of the Good Stuff – both foreign and autochthonous – of this quasi-omniscience of mine. I secured this feat through a judicious deployment of both the contemptuous curl of my lip and the conspicuous generosity of my bar bill.

We live in a self-obsessed age, so I should probably tell you a little about myself. This will test my literary skills to their limit, as there is little about me that may be considered interesting or exceptional, although I was brought up by doting parents to believe that I was precisely that. I have heard others speak enthusiastically of their own lives which were, quite unbelievably, even duller than my own. Isn't this the secret of our narcissistic culture: it feels no shame in publicising the trivial?

My name is Cinico de Oblivii and I was born in 1974 in the pleasant and undistinguished provincial town of Lugo di Romagna. My fellow townsfolk may take offence at this assertion, given that we have a castle in the main square and a spectacular eighteenth-century market called the Pavaglione, but in Italy this is nothing out of the ordinary. For all our stubbornly irresolvable problems, we have an architectural and artistic heritage second to none. In spite of my fancy Latin surname, my parents, like most Europeans, were in the main of peasant stock, and my father, always in search of significant forebears, could only trace the name back six generations to an orphanage, where the trail went cold. It was probably the invention of some monk or priest with an obscure sense of humour, and I'm happy with that interpretation, just as I'm happy to come from people who toiled and not from people who lived off that toil. None of this has held me back in the business of survival.

In my family history, there are no princes or counts, no generals or admirals, no captains of industry or discoverers of foreign lands and no celebrated artists or writers, yet I am sure that we could discover as many rogues, geniuses, adventurers, dreamers and saints as any other family, including those who could number those illustrious métiers back through the centuries.

Unlike my father I was never that interested and my knowledge is limited, but he was strangely unforthcoming about the one I wish to mention. Attilio de Oblivii, republican, socialist and follower of Mazzini and Garibaldi, lived a full life as they say. Some loved his harangues, but the right-thinking citizens of Lugo avoided him and the

8

taverns where he held court. In 1860, he left for Sicily in the second wave of Garibaldi's volunteers, and three thousand of these red shirts were transported by American naval vessels, demonstrating that even then the Land of the Free liked to meddle in other people's affairs – and to back whoever was likely to be the winner. Such was Attilio's loyalty to Garibaldi's cause that he took up arms again in 1862 when his leader visited Sicily and recruited an army to march up Southern Italy to liberate Rome. The Hero of Two Continents[1] was badly wounded by the army of the kingdom he had created, partly because he refused to open fire on soldiers he naively thought to be allies. Attilio had to make his way home on foot while avoiding the forces of order. On his return, he was more prudent in his anticlericalism because neither he nor the upholders of social norms knew that the pope's hold over the capital city would only last another nine years. After that happened Garibaldi spoke in many towns and cities, and Lugo was no exception. He gave a speech from a balcony in the main square to six hundred Lughese veterans according to a plaque on the castle wall, but more accurate records state that Attilio only had thirty-six comrades from his home town. Not that the six hundred weren't in the square listening to the leader they'd carelessly forgotten to follow in more difficult years, and Attilio, sensing perhaps that little was going to change, refused to join the post-revolutionary revolutionaries.

Having put my hero of two campaigns on a pedestal, I feel compelled to tell another story which may well knock him off it. Attilio married after Rome became Italian and had five children. Like everyone living on this planet, he grew

---

[1] The Hero of Two Continents: an antonomasia for Giuseppe Garibaldi, who fought for republican and secessionist regimes in Latin America, as well as for Italian independence and unification, and for the newly formed French Republic defending itself from the Prussian attack.

old and changed. The times of ideas and struggles were over, and he entered the times of hard work and financial worries. To maintain the creases in his trousers, he had them stitched, and to make his shoes last longer he hammered in tacks, as soldiers would do in the First World War, demonstrating where my father's misguided inventiveness may have come from. People could hear him coming, allowing the good burghers to retreat early and in good order, and during the winter snows he was constantly slipping over on the ice. Our oral traditions, just as reliable as any history books, record that he awoke one night and noticed that his wife was no longer breathing. Instead of shaking her gently or feeling her pulse, he knocked on the wall behind the bedstead and shouted to his son, Ettore, "Maria Assunta is no longer breathing, and I think she must be dead."

"Does this upset you, dad?" came the reply.

"No!"

"Well, let's sleep on it then, and we'll talk about it in the morning."

The next morning Maria Assunta rose from her bed as hale and hearty as she had ever been. Whether this was due to the divine intervention of the virgin she was named after or the idiocy and premature hopes of her husband has always been left to our varied intellectual inclinations and the matter was never satisfactorily resolved. The men in my family, being for the most part *mangiapreti*,[2] have always tended to the latter hypothesis, and this may explain why they speak so little of their heroic ancestor. Whenever I heard the story, I always thought how most of us, even rebels, belong entirely to our own times and those few who don't pay a high price.

My father was a schoolteacher and my mother had

---

[2]   *mangiapreti*: someone who is aggressively anticlerical, unlike *strozzapreti*, a particularly stodgy type of pasta whose literal meaning is "priest-chokers".

part-time secretarial work at a nearby chocolate factory at a time when there was secretarial work and the factory had not covered the globe with its tasteless adverts. They were both unremarkable, even when it came to my father's stubborn conviction that he was remarkable, indeed a genius ignored by an unperceptive society which might have consciously obstructed his career because it felt threatened by his brilliance. And quite unremarkably my mother conspired with him to perpetuate this absurd delusion, something she found so enervating and self-destructive that she died when I was in my early twenties. I doubt there is a scientifically recognised pathology for this condition but am certain that it exists; indeed it must have been very common amongst women of her generation. She considered the defence of her husband's conceits and fantasies to be one of her principal conjugal duties. Shared Marital Illusion Fatigue could be its name, generating of course the splendidly pronounceable acronym SMIF.

My father believed that he had invented cures for a number of animal maladies, both bovine and ovine, as well as having written an interminable chivalric poem in *ottava rima*,[3] as though Ludovico Ariosto had barely been laid to rest, painted a long series of landscapes in oil depicting an idealised view of the Italian countryside of his youth, and composed a new national anthem. Leaving aside the annihilation of an entire flock of sheep resulting from one of his serums, none of his self-imposed Herculean trials resulted in complete failure, but they avoided success just as surely. The flock of sheep, however, were decisive, and following a court case brought by the Sardinian owner of the unlucky herd, we lost our home and for several months had to live in nearby Russo to avoid the shame.

He was only successful in one cure: his behaviour

---

[3] *ottava rima*: term also used in English for the heroic rhyming scheme (ababacc), which Ariosto adopted.

unwittingly inoculated me against all creativity and sincerity. Such things may be admirable in others, but they are utterly ruinous to human happiness. Why become an expert in anything when the world is heaving with experts in everything – men and women who sacrificed their youth to expanding human understanding, and all in the name of progress. We should trust these licensed thinkers and distrust fantasists like my poor father.

When I heard a political argument start up, I didn't hear another word. I had heard it all before. Surely there was nothing more to be said. I felt, as do millions of others, that politicians are all in it for themselves. Whatever was said was tainted with subterfuge, and so it had been since Machiavelli's original sin – as usual we Italians were in there first, building the barriers to keep out the people who had been reading too many books and thinking up silly ideas no one could put into practice. We were midwives to the modern age whose disenchanted motto should be, "The powerful shall always be with us." Knock them down, and another identical group will take their place. Everything must change so that everything can stay the same. You know the stuff. Smoke and mirrors create a semblance of progress, but always money goes to money and power to power. There may be an occasional hiccup along the way, but that is the direction of travel.

It may seem surprising then that I ended up as a journalist and political commentator, but who would want a journalist who actually believed in something? Certainly not the paper I worked for. They wanted someone who followed every twist and turn in fashionable political truths, and I fitted the bill most perfectly. *Il Messaggio del Popolo* offered me the post of assistant politics reporter as soon as I left university in 1994. In this I was assisted by a well-connected professor, possibly because I flattered him in the knowledge that words cost nothing but a little effort. Or so

I thought.

It was like taking sweeties from a deaf and dumb toddler: the same skills I had perhaps unwittingly deployed against the university professor. I have always been proud of my native cunning, which often lacks any conscious process. I found that politicians differed very little from my father, except for the very decisive factor that their fantasies had become reality due, it seems, to a combination of happenchance and family connections. They shared my father's unshakable self-belief and self-love, which, for some strange reason, most people find attractive and reassuring. They shared my father's total disconnect from what was happening in the world and lived entirely within their own make-believe, which they conspired to uphold even beyond the distinctions of party and ideology. They spoke in an impenetrable jargon, which to some extent I had to learn and translate into the more demotic idiom of *Il Messaggio del Popolo*. As they all said more or less the same things, I had to spice up their empty outpourings and provide a little content of my own to compensate for what was missing. After a while, I found that not only the editor appreciated these creative flourishes but also the politicians themselves. I sometimes thought that they recycled my inventions in their next speech, but perhaps that was my own narcissism misleading me.

The fact is that my promotion was continuous. I was not a particularly ambitious man, but I liked my comforts and I liked to consume. Besides, if success came to me like a lover, why should I drive her from my bed? And lovers too came without difficulties, which makes it hard to explain the biggest mistake of my life: my marriage to a beautiful but vacuous woman. I was flattered, no doubt. The flatterer was caught in a snare no different from the ones he laid every day of his life, and I can now see a degree of poetic justice in all this, even though I was, for once, the victim. The marriage vows concluded, the flat in Monti bought and the mortgage documents signed, she metamorphosed into an unquenchable consumer and indefatigable socialite. Only then did I realise that she had nothing to tell me that was new, nothing to draw me into her company but her increasingly too familiar body, stunning as it was, and nothing to add to my life other than the envy of other men. In other words, she was as empty-headed as I was myself, and often, it is said, people who are very similar cannot live together for too long. We were of course very young; she may have become aware of her own vacuity in the meantime, just as I have of mine.

Then she became pregnant and in due course I became the troubled father of a troubled baby girl who never stopped screaming. By that time, fathers were all full of paternal love, but that fashion passed me by. All I felt was that my life had been invaded by obscure needs and unending drivel. And my carefree existence compromised. So it was that the editor and I agreed that a transfer to London would be in everyone's interests. The salary increase would allow my wife to continue her extravagant social life and pay for a Romanian woman to look after our daughter, who continued to display her cantankerous nature with unremitting verve. I could return to the pleasures of life in a new and fascinating environment. Tony Blair had been in power since 1997 and his particular brand of snake oil was all the rage. The first rumblings of a war in Iraq could be heard. The editor wanted a reliable and energetic reporter there, because he mistakenly thought that I was energetic, whilst in fact I worked very little and was skilful at winging it. At last everyone was happy and I left for London.

II

I Make my Acquaintance of the Professor

Life in London was a pleasant change from the incestuous humdrum and interminable inconclusiveness of Italian politics. Politics in Britain was no less corrupt than in Italy, but occasionally something was actually decided upon that didn't concern the private life or finances of politicians themselves. There was a buzz about the place because the British had started to delude themselves that they mattered once more. Our empire died one and a half millennia ago, and we have long since got over the loss, but the British were still hurt by their diminished status. They felt that they had invented a wonderful kind of economy in which it was no longer necessary to produce anything; it was sufficient to move money around imaginatively. And some of them longed to return to the international stage, which they could only achieve through a close and subservient relationship with the United States. But London gave me something infinitely more important than any of these things: anonymity.

I was free not only of my new family but also my old one, which by then had long been reduced to my increasingly irascible and deluded father. He made demands on my finances of course, because he was incapable of dealing with life, but, much worse, he insisted on interfering in my life and passing judgement on my own decisions, which generally speaking I made with very little judgement of my own. Nevertheless I was much more successful and self-sufficient than he had ever been. Naturally I felt these intrusions to be more than a little irritating, even though I was well practised in the business of being irritated by my father. In London I discovered immediately how pleasurable it is not to have a father living merely a short train journey away.

London, however, had more to offer when it came to anonymity: it has a whole lifestyle based on anonymity, as I was to discover. It is a city distinguished by a genial, even genteel, detachment. What we call *menefreghismo*[4] – not caring about other people. We have this interesting word for it, because we have to work at it; it doesn't come naturally. They, on the other hand, consider it to be the natural state for human beings, at least in the circles I moved in, which were certainly not representative of anything but the indigenous professional class. In fact, they had invented a philosophy to prove that this is our natural state, and called it utilitarianism.

London has its drawbacks, and in spite of a few very good restaurants, the food is generally deplorable. They take more care of the petrol they put in their cars than the comestibles they put in their bodies. It is no more than a fuel for them. A distraction. Drinking alcohol, on the other hand, is treated as a necessary task, a challenge, an exercise, like climbing a mountain or going for a long walk. Many like to keep a mental record of the various drinks they have consumed in an evening, as though each were a victorious battle in a military campaign. I was an avowed hedonist and never refused a good wine or whisky, but I could see little pleasure in this continuous assault on mind and body. I soon decided to abstain from their unending Bacchic festivities and, as is typical of my nature, preferred to stay up late and scrutinise their antics with sociological thoroughness. It appeared to me that Londoners and perhaps the British in general reveal that they do care about each other and occasionally hate each other when under

---

[4] *menefreghismo*: a crude Italian abstract noun for not caring; it derives from Me ne frego! which was popularised by Fascism as a slogan and means "I couldn't care a fuck!"

the influence of alcohol. Their humanity, which is usually concealed, comes out with extra force and disproves their preferred philosophy of life.

Another surprising aspect of middle-class Londoners is that they appear to have extremely weak vocal chords. By nature somewhat taciturn, when they speak it is barely above a whisper. I found myself constantly having to strain my ears and at one point thought that I might have been going deaf. Some of those who have been to what they call public schools can be very loud, and given the low volume of their colleagues, they seem even louder. I soon learnt to avoid the louder ones, who can be boorish in the extreme. Loudness in Italy seems inclusive and hospitable, but in London it seems exclusive and arrogant. It tells others to keep quiet, and usually they do.

I'm not one of those who travel abroad with an air of inexhaustible and contemptuous surprise at the predictable otherness of other nations, as do many Italians. Why, some say, do the British insist on having those clunky plugs and sockets? Why not? I reply, they do their job no better and no worse than ours do. I like their clunkiness, which the British probably perceive as robustness. Why travel, if you dislike diversity and a different feel to the texture of life? And under that pleasant and intriguing exterior, you'll find that the human condition is unchanged, with all that is good and bad in that.

Of course, some things are done better at home and some things better in Britain. Why, for instance, do the British have two taps on most of their basins in public lavatories, so that you have to either burn your hands or freeze them? I don't mind them either. The trick is to rinse your hands before the water becomes really hot. Don't these minor tribulations add something to our lives? Going to Britain is hardly living dangerously, although a little indigestion is inevitable.

I have to admit that the years I lived in London felt very enjoyable at the time, although I now often think of them

17

as wasted. Surely wasted years are not really wasted, particularly if you enjoyed them. While I pursued a life of unadulterated selfishness, I was in fact learning something, and unconsciously tiring myself of greed. London in the early twenty-first century was a good place to be greedy – it was, I believe, a more sophisticated greediness, precisely because it was not where the real power lay.

It is not of my London days that I want to write. Late in 2013, I received an e-mail from the editor requesting that I spend time in Edinburgh to follow the Scottish referendum. I had heard of Scotland before coming to Britain, but I never took its existence very seriously. The English did not speak ill of that country; it very rarely came up in conversation. I was vaguely aware of the north of England, which the South despises. Scotland was, in my opinion, no different from the many other small states that had disappeared, such as Bavaria, the Grand-Duchy of Tuscany, the Kingdom of Naples, and Aragon, the first three of which had survived for much longer than it had. Like most Italians, I was in the habit of calling all the inhabitants of Great Britain *inglesi* or English. I also had an Italian's distrust of nationalism, as I found the Lega Nord ridiculous, with their green uniforms and absurd xenophobia. I didn't know that what was happening in Scotland was very different.

I needed a guide to get me up to speed on these provincial politicians, and *Il Messaggio del Popolo* provided for this too. They put me in touch with George Lovenight, the professor of politics at East of Scotland University. It was friendship at first sight, because I believed Professor Lovenight to be both practical and concerned, informed and flexible, sensible and moral. For me, good had always meant success, the evasion of failure, which is always *in agguato*,[5] and of course,

---

[5] *in agguato*: the nearest translation may be "ready to pounce", but this is not entirely satisfactory.

bella figura.[6] I was to discover during the unusual events I witnessed during my Scottish sojourns that this favourite opinion of mine, which I proudly declaimed as though it were proof of my intellectual acuity, was, at the very least, shallow and destructive.

Lovenight was slightly below average height, slightly overweight and slightly deaf, and approaching fifty years of age with a tendency to breathlessness. And of course, the obligatory bifocals. He was, as an academic, entirely unremarkable, although it's true that many academics of his generation spend more time climbing hills than reading books, and he was not one of them. He was reassuringly professorial and loved to ramble on with no apparent direction to his thoughts, which for an Italian can be incredibly *simpatico*,[7] though not so for the British, who admire the succinct and businesslike. So he had a listener, and I had a source from which to pour out as much garbage as the editor could take. It was a professional marriage made in heaven.

We met in a café close to Edinburgh University. I had insisted, because I was beginning to find pubs oppressive and soulless, and besides I was not familiar with any in the Scottish capital. The coffee was not bad, and there was room to sit. He appeared to be in a rush and a little put out at having to educate a foreign journalist, which for some reason only increased my deference to him, but once he sat down, he couldn't stop talking and showed little sign of having other commitments. Life for the modern middle classes is truly an agreeable and diverting one; it is well remunerated often for doing things that might be considered leisure activities. We started with the pleasantries,

---

[6] *bella figura*: this term already has some currency in English because it is not just showmanship (principally male showmanship), but also the philosophy or culture that underlies it.

[7] *simpatico*: "likable" or "agreeable" are probably the best translations in this context.

which we practise everywhere but in a different manner. In Britain, it's necessary to restrict them to the totally banal. A Frenchman said that when two Englishmen meet they discuss the weather. The Scots are no different, and in the presence of an Italian the British always feel that they have to praise our weather, as though it were the same in all our regions and unremittingly sunny. Wine. Food. Berlusconi. The state of the Venetian lagoon. His holiday at Lago di Garda, and the awfulness of President Chirac. I'd heard it all before in England, but for some reason he charmed me. He seemed reassuringly civilised and accepting of other people's views, which was easy to do in my case as I had none of my own. He expressed his concerns for immigrants and his attachment to women's rights. He cared, while I was what? A man without a care, I would say. Or a man whose only care was to take good care of himself.

He set out the background to the political conflict that had been brewing in Scotland for some time. The Labour Party, he explained, had attempted to establish a devolved parliament as far back as 1979, but unfortunately the Scots hadn't voted for it. The party tried again in 1997 and succeeded. Since then the nationalists had been alluring Labour voters with false promises, but the Scottish electorate would never abandon their traditional allegiances in spite of minor successes for the nationalists. A crushing defeat of the Yes campaign would marginalise the SNP once more. Nationalism was a regressive and inward-looking movement, which was tantamount to turning one's back on the world – suicide in a global economy. Hence the appropriateness of the No campaign's brief slogan: Better Together.

"The problem with Britain," said Lovenight, who, almost from the beginning I started to refer to as the good professor in my contacts with the paper and indeed in my head, "is that it has become too tolerant. It is now guilty of what we can only call passive tolerance. For too long we have been saying to our citizens and more especially to those who come to live amongst us that we'll leave them alone as long as they obey the law. By doing this we have abdicated our right to protect our own quite unique values."

"And is New Labour standing up for those values, then?" I asked almost instinctively, because I knew this language. We have it in Italy too.

"We don't call it New Labour any more," he digressed with wonderful adroitness at not answering the question, "simply because New Labour has been around so long that it has become Labour. No one wants to return to the bad old days when we neglected aspirational voters and hardworking families."

I was confused. Surely all voters hope for some improvement in their lives or even the lives of others, though it isn't always a financial one, as some believe. Isn't the very act of voting expressing yet again the victory of hope over experience? That human folly that occasionally trips up even inveterate cynics like myself.

Happy with my takings, I returned to my hotel. I'm an ace at translating the offerings of men and women like George Lovenight into column inches in my newspaper, which people can read, even if when they get to the end of the article they may feel that they've heard most of it before. The two forms of translation – from English into Italian and from politickese into journalese – worked in tandem, and in no time I had completed a couple of long articles mixing verbatim with my fertile stock of platitudes and the odd nugget picked off *Wikipedia*. I e-mailed them to the paper, and the rest of the evening was my own.

III

What the Edinburgh Academic Had to Say

I have always liked Edinburgh, as one might a slightly stuffy but also feisty non-consanguineous aunt of a higher social rank than one's own. There is an affection of adoptive kinship but also a distance of wealth and culture – or at least the appearance of those things.

On the professor's instructions I went to see Jane Macpherson. He had told me that she knew all I needed to know about Scottish literature and culture. She was head of the English literature department at Edinburgh University, and I was ushered into her office as though to a royal audience, which to anyone used to Italian universities is nothing strange, but somewhat out of kilter with the studied informality of British higher education.

"Italian?" she asked me, as though she were referring to some unfortunate condition. I thought that the good professor would have given her my details in quintuplicate, as was his habit.

"Yes," I replied with an equal measure of brevity.

"I see, and you want to know about Scottish literature? I can't imagine why."

"Professor Lovenight thought it would be a good idea."

"Typical."

At this stage, I thought that the interview was going to be difficult and not very productive. Nevertheless I was hooked: here was someone who was different – utterly her own self – and discovering who she was going to be, at the very least, congenial.

"He's in the habit of sending you Italians?"

"Not at all. You are stupid. He can send me as many

Italians as he likes; I just wish that he wouldn't send me journalists, who, you'll forgive me, are hardly likely to entertain. They feed on your words, fail to understand them and then regurgitate them in abysmal prose." I sympathised with her point of view. I never thought that my profession was a worthy or even useful one, as so many journalists do. We deal in lies and subterfuge at the bidding of our masters. We are hacks. I felt it important not to show offence, nor indeed did I feel any.

"You're not entirely wrong, I have to admit. We do not seek the truth so much as information with which to decorate a preconceived truth."

She chuckled, "You'll have me believe there's an honest journalist at last. Be careful, I'm keeping an eye on you. You must be a slippery one." To emphasise the point, she looked at me fiercely over her reading glasses, which she had not removed, presumably to communicate that this was going to be a short interview.

"I have to confess that I know very little. Of your literature I've only read Stevenson's *Treasure Island*, which I read in an abridged version when I was seven."

"Really?" she stared at me, searching for something she might have missed on the other occasions she had stared at me. "I don't have long, you know. What exactly do you want to know? I could just say go to your nearest bookshop and buy some novels by James Kelman, Alasdair Gray and Allan Massie, as well as some poems by Norman MacCaig. It's not enough, but it's a start. Oh, and leave me in peace."

"I was more interested in defining what is distinctive about Scottish literature and culture in the context of the Scottish referendum."

"In the context of? You certainly talk like a journalist, and you want me to do your job for you?"

The answer was clearly yes, but inappropriate in her presence. I felt that I could get something interesting from her once she stopped playing games.

23

"I'm afraid that I'm here for the referendum. It's my job," I adopted the apologetic tone of the supplicant.

"That's all very well, but I'm not a professor of politics, unlike your friend George Lovenight. I care very little about the referendum, which has gone on for far too long. If the Scots are stupid enough to vote for independence, then so be it. It's not my concern, and I have no expertise in these matters." Clearly she found political debate shabby and dis-tasteful, and although she almost certainly had well-developed political ideas of her own, she didn't want to share them with passing trade.

"Is there such a thing as a distinctive Scottish literature and culture?"

"Well that's a damn fool question to start with. Of course there is. It is just as distinctive as any other literature or culture, but literature in particular is literature because it doesn't stay within its own borders. Literature doesn't belong to a nation; it belongs to everyone. This has noth-ing to do with the referendum, which is about political independence. You must know this: under the Austro-Hungarian Empire, Trieste was not only a thriving com-mercial centre; it was a significant centre of Italian culture. After it became part of Italy, as so many writers and artists wanted, it was turned into a provincial backwater. You can never guess what effects political events will have on cul-tures. The defeat of the Gaelic world at Culloden led to the greatest flowering of Gaelic poetry. Culture has its own cycles and dynamics, and rarely acts predictably."

"You refer to such writers as Svevo and Saba?"

"So you have read a few books. Pity that they're only Italian ones."

I refused to be provoked. Italians are much more likely to read foreign literatures than the British are, and I'm no exception. "What then is this referendum about?"

"I would have thought that it is obvious. It's about class. Too many people in Scotland are in search of a meal ticket.

Britain can't afford that, and they think that Scotland with its oil can. They're mistaken. This referendum is just another puerile anti-establishment campaign."

"You support the establishment?" I was surprised because the British middle classes are not normally so forthright.

"Why shouldn't I? I come from the establishment. The establishment is necessary. Get rid of this one, and you'll just get another one, which will probably be worse. Why bother?"

I was a little mystified, though hardly in disagreement, and said, "George Lovenight doesn't support the establishment. Perhaps it's not politically correct."

"George Lovenight is just as much the establishment as I am, with the not insignificant difference that I am the old establishment and he is the new one. I am not interested in what is and isn't politically correct. Now look what you've done: you've got me talking politics in the afternoon, which is not something I'm in the habit of doing, let me tell you.

"Now, if you're not going to talk about literature, I suggest you leave, Mr De Oblivii, taking your ridiculous surname with you."

Jane Macpherson's advice is of the kind most sane men would wish to follow, and after shaking her hand as warmly as I could to show no hard feelings, I left. Everything she had said was interesting, and utterly useless from a professional point of view.

So if Edinburgh became a woman, she would resemble the *signora* Macpherson quite closely. A city "all of one piece", as we say in Italy,[8] Edinburgh is both handsome and aloof, but capable of communicating some quite complex things, as every capital city should: its elitism is not wholly undemocratic, its primness is not without self-awareness, and its middle-class smugness is compensated for by a vast

---

[8]   *tutto d'un pezzo* in the original

array of purveyors of the worst tat, which in a small city like Edinburgh can feel overwhelming. For a long time, I thought that "tat" was never dissociated from "tartan".

We really got to work in January of 2014, with eight months to go before the referendum. The Yes vote looked to be far behind, but their supporters were much more active, though less so in Edinburgh. My overall impression of the referendum battle was that the No supporters did very little campaigning in the streets, and relied almost entirely on their almost unanimous support in the mass media. In other words, the No campaign was a modern one, and the Yes campaign a throwback to the sixties and seventies when public meetings were held across the country. This trend must have been almost universal across Europe, with the possible exception of France, and now Scotland was attempting to reverse it. Even then I sensed a boldness in all this, but whether it was a quixotic interlude or a new chapter in our European history was a question I still failed to asked myself.

Lovenight's methodology was to introduce me to as many experts as possible, and experts, we all know, like to gather in the capital where the pickings are much richer. They were meat and drink to me, even though they were intolerably resistant to saying anything that differed dramatically from the dominant narrative. I started going to public meetings on my own, and they confirmed Macpherson's observation of the class nature of this electoral struggle. I went to a miners' club in the east of Edinburgh to hear Jim Paterson, a particularly active campaigner for the Yes campaign. The question and answer opened not with a question but a fiery speech from a middle-aged man whose anger flowed from a copious spring. He appeared to round on everyone, both in the room and in the campaign outside. Not enough was being done on any front, and betrayal was everywhere. He ended his harangue by leaving the hall and slamming the door behind him. As an Italian, I found it strange that no one referred to him either from the panel or from the floor. Perhaps they, like me, understood very little of what he said, and all I learned from it was the passion that strangely coexisted with calm civility.

During the main speech Paterson mentioned, as he often did, a plan he had for an independent Scotland. The new country would take one of the aircraft carriers then under construction and convert it into a hospital ship to tour the coasts of the Third World and provide free healthcare to populations that had none. This idea of replacing military might with humanity electrified the working-class audience, who would frequently refer to it in their questions. A sense of potential pride was already there, and the idea of a nation that they would mould into something generous and different. It was a moment that shared emotion and ideas, and even someone as hard-headed as I am could not fail to be affected, though my immediate reaction was to push that distrusted emotion away. A few weeks later I attended a similar event with Paterson in the middle-class district of Bruntsfield, which is close to the university, and amongst the audience there was an archbishop I had met at an arts event. I fully expected a similar or even stronger reaction from these good people to the story of the converted aircraft carrier, but when it came it passed entirely unnoticed or at least it engendered no intakes of breath or expressions of excitement, not even from the man whose life's work had been to guide his flock along the path of a pacifist religion. I'm not so unusual then: the middle class in general is dismissive of all fantasies of a better world. We know how the real thing works and what its limitations are. The market requires confidence and certainty, not irrational altruism.

To understand this hyperactive Yes campaign more fully, I needed to travel further, but I resisted as I became increasingly familiar with the Scottish capital, whilst also returning south to my London flat as my work dictated. Fortunately decisions were to be made for me.

IV

What the Glasgow Hardman and
the Ukrainian Had to Say

The editor's voice, generally friendly and a pleasure to hear, was beginning to annoy me. Things were not going well at the paper. Falling circulation and falling revenues from advertising were more than discomforting him. Back at the office, which thankfully I had left behind, it was becoming a rush to stay in the same place – it was running the wrong way up an escalator. As long as they kept me stationed in Britain, I was almost immune to that panic, and perhaps there was also a little envy in his tone of voice.

"Cinico," he said without his usual niceties, "you need to get the big story. What you're sending me is fine, but it's becoming repetitious. If you want to keep going up there, you have to find a different angle – and a different hotel."

"A different hotel?"

"That's right; one that costs less."

"They're much of a muchness."

"Well, I was meaning to say that you've got to get out into the country. What kind of a place is this Scotland? The real place. Not the castles and whisky we all know about. There must be some people living up there in the cold mists,[9] heaven help them: get out and interview them. And the hotels will be cheaper. That's the bonus for me."

"You've no idea what it's like. And I'm not a travel writer."

---

[9] *tra le brume*: "in the mists", often used as a pejorative for northern climes.

"Versatility is the watchword of the day, my friend. I'm not asking; I'm telling you."

"That's going to be a lot of nights."

"Then take that professor as your guide, and do it in less. He's not that expensive. I think that he likes being the fixer; *fa bella figura*, it seems. He has a job that pays well, and which he appears to neglect. That's *statali*[10] for you."

A change is better than a relaxing holiday, which is usually oppressively dull. This could become an entertaining little romp. The professor could do the work, and I could do what I do best – chatter away, entertain and seduce the odd woman *en passant*. I had the idea that the *cicaline*[11] in rural Scotland could be horribly Calvinistic and difficult to get at, but with my Italian bravado, I liked a challenge.

The professional challenge was more concerning. What was the big story? Was I supposed to root around until I came across it by chance, or was I supposed to manufacture it and fit the facts around it? The latter seemed the more likely, but the intellectual effort was not enticing.

The relationship between industrial or post-industrial Glasgow and the capital Edinburgh is a little like the one between Milan and Rome. Glasgow is larger and does more than Edinburgh, even if it no longer has any heavy industry. Like Milan, it spills out of its own territory and into conjoining council areas and then into various dormitory towns that create a much larger conurbation. It is brasher,

---

[10] *statali*: collective noun for all state-funded employees.

[11] *cicaline*: this vulgar term for attractive young women is very dated, and now almost completely supplanted by another similar one. There is something old-fashioned about Cinico, as though he emulates his parents' generation even as he berates them endlessly. Given that his views are supposed to mature over the period of this account, there may be some self-irony or even self-deprecation in this portrayal of his behaviour and attitudes.

more vital than Milan and in some ways less sure of itself. It is a bourgeois and proletarian city in the strict sense of the terms, and its opposing classes are equally proud of the city, although it could be argued that the cities they are proud of are not the same.

However, in some ways the relationship is reversed: Glasgow and Rome are the loud and chaotic cities, and Milan and Edinburgh are the staid and orderly ones. Glasgow is a city in which an Italian can feel at home. They share a degree of our theatricality, and are talkative and very keen to know other people's business, while being far from reticent when speaking of their own. They drive like us too. Some of their citizens are in fact of Italian origin: the city has a very large population of Irish origin, but the Catholic component also includes a not insignificant number of Italians. The Glasgow vernacular is very different, and in spite of my many years in Britain, in its purest form I find it completely impenetrable.

George had arranged for me to meet a leading figure in the Glasgow Labour Party and the No campaign. He was apparently more a mover and shaker than a front-line politician – a man who dealt with politicians and presumably bullied them into doing what was required. David Finlayson was heavily built, and had the presence of an armoured car parked in your garden with its canon pointed at your sitting room. You wanted to run but you couldn't abandon your home – or be seen to do that. He looked not so much the ex-student of a school of hard knocks as the founder of one. And his physiognomy was more sandstone than granite, given that bits appeared to have fallen off it. I knew instantly that if our two heads were to collide under whatever force, only mine would be damaged. From the lump of his face, two blue eyes shone improbably with a cautious intelligence.

George greeted the man as though he were a long-lost brother, which surprised me because Lovenight was not prone to effusiveness. I would have thought them comrades in a criminal activity, were it not for George's exemplary moral probity. When the professor introduced me, Finlayson grunted without a glance in my direction. If I had just arrived in Britain for the first time, this would have bothered me. In Scotland such behaviour is more extreme than in England – more explicit. In fact Scots are a people of extremes, as are Italians but in a different way. Scots can be laconic, as with Mr Finlayson, or loquacious. They can drink alcohol from noon to night or never touch a drop – and in both cases they do this with fervour. They can be generous to a fault or as tight as the world unfairly believes them to be. We Italians, on the other hand, are more extreme with the prevailing ideas of our times: we were first in with fascism, predominantly Christian Democrat after the war, the most left-wing in the sixties and seventies, the most apathetic in the eighties and nineties, and the most subject to the *qualunquismo*[12] first of Berlusconi and then of Cinque Stelle. But through it all, our main business was something else: living, loving, eating, talking aimlessly and convivially – a Mediterranean culture.

"David, I've brought Cinico here to see you because he wants to know more about our referendum," George often spoke in the tone of a chairman introducing a meeting.

"He does, does he?" Finlayson said with the voice of someone who had chewed pebbles for breakfast, and clearly spoke without hairs on his tongue.[13]

---

[12] *qualunquismo*: could be translated as "whateverism", a term used to describe populism and demagoguery. It derives from a political movement of this kind which was active in the immediate post-war period for less than a decade.

[13] "spoke without hairs on his tongue": this translation of the original *parlava senza peli sulla lingua* is literal. I think that it is clear: he was straight-talking, his conversation was not impeded by the niceties of good society or what are sometimes called distortions and lies.

"Yes, he's really interested …"

"He could try reading the newspapers. He speaks English, doesn't he?"

"Very well actually. He's been the London correspondent of *Il Messaggio del Popolo* for many years."

"Not exactly the fucking *Corriere della Sera!*" Finlayson proved to have an unexpected knowledge of how things stood.

"Come on, David, stop mucking around."

I thought that this might be the moment to take a diplomatic grip of the situation and demonstrate my command of the English language and unintentionally my Italian wordiness: "Mr Finlayson, I appreciate that you're a busy man, but George explained that you're the expert on this matter, and so I took the liberty of insisting on meeting with you as soon as possible. My editor says that our readers are really fascinated by what's happening here in Scotland."

He turned to me, stared at me for what felt like an unpleasantly long period of time and then started the even more unpleasantly cumbersome task of rearranging his mouth into what vaguely resembled a smile. Only after this delicate operation was complete, did he say in a slightly higher and less gravelly voice, "He does? No wonder your paper's circulation figures are falling all the time. D'ye get me, mister Italian journalist?"

I could have replied, "Yes I do, mister Glasgow politician," but instead it was, "David, we're all busy men, why don't we get down to business?"

With a look of distaste, Finlayson turned back to the professor: "What does he want to know, then?"

"Cinico wants to know why we should stay together with the English."

"I hate the fucking English, …"

"Come come, David, Mr De Oblivii is from Italy, …"

"… but I hate the SNP even more, and as for that numpty Alex Salmond, they should go away and bile his heid."

"You don't really believe that ..."

"George, how many times have I said it when there wasnae an Italian journalist present, and you never complained then?"

I tried again to intervene: "I don't object, but I would like to know why."

"Okay, mister Italian journalist, I'll tell you why without the bullshit. Nothing you write is going to matter a flying fuck in this referendum. This is a bit of local trouble that'll be forgotten in six months. It's a non-event, but this is my take on it: I've worked nearly all my adult life for the labour movement and if the Yes side wins, the SNP wins. If the SNP wins, the Labour Party is deid in the water, get it? They're already in power in our make-pretendy parliament; if they got their sticky mits on a real one, nobody knows where we'd end up. There's a Tory-led coalition in London, the economy's fucked and we're the only ones capable of defending working people."

"But surely ..."

"Mister Italian journalist, don't come here and tell us how to run the country. We've had enough of people doing that in the past. They days are over."

After these two meetings, I was coming to the conclusion that the good professor wasn't always good at finding me people who could give me the kind of information I could quickly recycle to meet my deadlines. But he often was, and that band of soothsayers was the subject of too many of my articles to find a place in these pages. The interesting and colourful people, the eccentrics and outliers would prove to be of some use in the run-up to polling day – when a broader understanding of the conflicts and prejudices was needed to some extent, but here finally come into their own. They're the people I want to write about now.

Later George put aside his professorial voice and apologised. Finlayson was not having a good day, he explained unconvincingly. The politician was, to my mind, no fool but foolish enough to believe in the unrestricted power of his own cleverness. He would only open up when it was necessary. If not, his default was to drive away all people who had no usefulness. Finlayson was perfectly in control of himself, and measured his nonchalance very carefully.

After the meeting with Finlayson, I took the subway – as they call it in Glasgow – to my hotel on the Southside. That day nothing seemed to reassure. I was standing on the platform in Buchanan Street subway station, happy with how my trip to Scotland was going. To be honest, it looked to me then to be a bit of a backwater, but one that I could enjoy for a brief spell. Now it's the concept of backwater that seems obsolete, and familiarising it has changed me. The scale in Scotland is small, except the public buildings which sometimes seem assertive beyond their reach. Most people live in or close to the four largest cities, and great stretches of land are empty or nearly empty. Like all nations, Scotland is no monolith – not the homogeneous reality suggested by stereotypes – and like all nations it has something distinctive that holds it together. Then I felt that I could understand it in a few months, and when I left, I felt that were I to live there for another twenty years I still wouldn't be able to do so. Not, I think, because Scotland is a particularly hard nut to crack, but because all nations are. Even my own, which I now understand better having lived abroad and developed something to judge it against, feels more inscrutable than before.

A young, professional, South Asian couple came down the steps to the platform. They were laughing, and appeared to be a picture of relaxed familiarity: brother and sister perhaps, but more likely man and wife, or lovers. Then the woman stopped and turned towards the rails to await the train, and the man moved on in his own world, still chortling to himself. He too turned towards the rails, as though performing a choreographed daily ritual that required no consciousness.

They were, it would now appear at least, entirely separate individuals who for a fraction of time were level with each other, but never exchanged a glance. The laughter was unshared and its concurrence coincidental. I asked myself whether I would have made this mistake, had they been white, and convinced myself that I would have. I've often holidayed in India, and know the country well in the superficial manner of a tourist. I would go so far as to say that I prefer Indians to bloated Europeans, including Italians, and Indian English to the English spoken by the English; they inject a little life into that listless language. Humour and unfathomable conceits linger in their lilted tones, but Asian Scots were less remarkable. Or rather these ones were, as they were talking and laughing to themselves and no one was noticing. They were European, and surely I had to know them and understand them. I was proud of my ability to assess every detail at a glance, and disliked it when I got it wrong. But how much do you see when you only glance at things with a knowing eye?

I got on the tube, as they call it in London, but these Glasgow trains are like toys in their orange livery: the clockwork orange is a local name. As it clattered along in truly clockwork fashion, I noticed the young woman in front of me. She sat straight-backed and prim, holding her handbag awkwardly upright on her knees. She was a picture of Presbyterian repression, and my Latin temperament soon had me fantasising about her body in my arms. I would defrost her northern aloofness, which I thought of as an act of charity. She was not unattractive, in spite of a certain ungainliness. Then in the midst of my fantasies, her phone rang and with unexpected alacrity she whipped it out of that inelegant bag, flicking it open as she did, and with a huge smile that ran from ear to ear she started to talk quickly and excitedly. "You're a dark horse," she said and giggled. "Now stop that, or I'll have to hose you down, you daft bugger." And on and on it went, and for some reason, I blushed in embarrassment, while a disturbing thought entered my head. What had she thought of me, when I was fitting her to a national stereotype? Did she consider me "a shit in a suit", an expression I had heard in those parts? Did she guess my Italianness and more importantly did she guess my thoughts? Or did she even notice me? Up until her phone call I was comfortably certain of my attraction to women, but now that certainty was shaken for some irrational reason, which may have been the discovery of the limitations to my own reason. After all, seduction is primarily about understanding human beings or rather women in my case: knowing how far to go, and judging the reactions. These are skills that are honed over the years, and suddenly I was no longer sure of them.

Perhaps, I wondered, I had not understood the Asian Scots because they were Scots and not because they were Asians. I expect Asian culture to be different, and I approach it with curiosity but also with tact, while I expect to find all Europeans tractable. Yes, we can joke about how much the British and the Germans drink, we can scoff at each other's accents, but ultimately we are all Europeans. All Christians, all grandchildren of the Roman Empire. We think in a similar way, we share the same stories and conceits. We have killed for the same conflicting ideals through history, and we've been brutalised by the same internecine strife over centuries: wars of religion, revolutions, imperial campaigns which took our bloodletting elsewhere, and massacres motivated by ideology and xenophobia. We should know each other by now.

And so I thought, when I lived in my comfortable bubble in London. Only on that day travelling along the Glasgow subway did I realise that I didn't know London at all. I knew a professional elite that is now European, and at least bilingual – though not of course the monoglot British amongst us, the majority. We foreigners speak English and our own languages, and we move in an increasingly uniform continental culture – itself becoming part of something global. It occurred to me that I didn't misunderstand the young woman because she was Scottish, but because she didn't belong to the elite. Why was this happening? Perhaps because the referendum was such an awakening that it was bringing me into contact with people I wasn't in the habit of meeting. Because I was unsettled by this experience, I was looking at the world as though for the first time, and studying all its details as I had never done before. I was discovering that people didn't behave as I expected them to, but in another time and place they would have passed by unnoticed. And with each layer of the onion I peeled away, I encountered another intractable misunderstanding. Above all, it was Europe that I didn't understand – that is the Europe outside the cosmopolitan elite. Could it be that the cosmopolitans live in the smallest village of all? Could it be that elites believe only they can nurture their finer human sentiments and therefore only they can be trusted with responsibility, while basing this conceit on a complete absence of knowledge or experience?

Out of the subway, I decided to take a walk in a small park nearby which I had noticed on my way from the hotel in the morning. I came across a play area where a blond, heavily built young man was doing an inordinate number of pull-ups on a child's climbing frame and counting them in his own language. A bearded man in a woolly hat stopped playing with his children and stared at the man's effortless exercising, clearly fascinated by such profligate expenditure of energy.

"Where are you from?" he asked the foreigner – that predictable question which can be motivated by either friendly curiosity or distrust. The man stopped counting and, by way of a response, dropped gracefully, landing with a bending of the knees and a reciprocal leap into the air before announcing – proudly, I thought – "Ukraine."

He glowed with good health and I felt that I was in the presence of a well-trained animal – something that made me a little uneasy.

"So how d'ye like it here in Scotland?" the woolly hat asked genially, and I noticed that he said Scotland and not Britain or the UK.

"It is good. I like England, and I am working for large British multinational that makes pumps. Six-month secondment."

If the woolly hat had not been wearing a woolly hat, I'm sure that I would have seen his hair bristle. "Ye're no in England, pal!" he said with a tinge of aggression – mindful of the Ukrainian's spectacular biceps which shone in the late-winter light, as he was wearing a T-shirt.

The Ukrainian plainly didn't understand and stood like a man hypnotised.

"You're in Scotland; you're not in England," the woolly hat explained in slower and more standard English, while his children called to him to start turning the roundabout again. They had been waiting patiently since the scene began to unfold.

"But Scotland is not country, I think," the Ukrainian said as though there were no argument.

"Aye, mebbie, but it will be on the 18th of September."

Again the Ukrainian looked lost for words: "The 18th of September?"

"Yes, the 18th of September. The referendum. We're going to leave the United Kingdom."

"Of course, the referendum. No one thinks that this is going to happen. I have lots of English friends at pump factory. I am educated man. I have MA."

The woolly hat was no longer interested, and the conversation could have ended there. "Aye well, nobody knows, but my money's on Yes."

The Ukrainian was now more interested in the conversation than was the woolly hat: "Why do you not want to be in England? What has it done wrong?"

"The list's too long to tell ye, pal. We'd be here all day."

"One thing," the Ukrainian challenged him.

The woolly hat sighed and smiled. "Where do I start?" he asked himself, and perhaps he would have started on a list but something else occurred to him – a light bulb in a balloon: "Why did Ukraine leave Russia?"

"Because they were communists."

"But so were you, and besides the Russians had just stopped being communists too."

The Ukrainian looked confused again, and I was now the one intrigued. I opened the gate to the play area and took a few steps towards them. "Russians," he replied, "are bad people. Everyone knows that in the West. Russia is backward country. You don't know that?"

"Some Ukrainians want to be part of Russia. Others want the impossible: they want their Soviet Union back."

The Ukrainian did not understand much, I think, but enough to get angry. "You have no right to make our decisions. If we want to be part of Europe, that is our decision. You have no right ..."

"I never said I had a right. Ukraine for the Ukrainians, I would say. But you haven't made that decision. You elected one president and then overthrew him in a coup with a little help from your friends in America, no doubt. If we'd had thirty policemen shot in Trafalgar Square, the police would have responded with much greater force. Without a single policeman being shot, our police have killed – even a newsagent leaving his work oblivious to the reasons for the demonstration itself. People cried out for justice, but no one that I recall called for the government to be overturned by violence or even for it to resign. The governments in the breakaway states of Eastern Ukraine are just as legitimate as the one in Kiev."

The Ukrainian, disadvantaged by his meagre command of English – serviceable for work and the polite middle-class gatherings he probably frequented, but unequal to the current talk – was silent once more.

The woolly hat, on the other hand, was getting into his stride, though his children were silent, even fearful, with those antennae they have that pick up signals we sometimes miss, even though they cannot understand. "What about the Russian speakers in the east and the south that were never part of historic Ukraine: the east being Russian and the south being Ottoman until it was Russified in the seventeenth and eighteenth centuries? Surely they have as much right to secede as Ukraine did from Russia?"

The Ukrainian was up against a well-informed ball-buster,[14] and in the other man's language. He responded with his principal weapon: his presence. He walked up to the woolly hat, the synecdoche who barely reached up to his neck, and there was half a metre between them. "I have nothing against those people, but they cannot stand in our way. I have MA, you know. Those are not educated people, and we need to educate them. You, Scottishman, cannot understand this because you are not Ukrainian. You should mind your own business."

The woolly hat turned on his heels and walked back to his children whom he herded gently and quietly out of the play area. And I walked hastily away, conscious once more of how brute force is usually the winning argument – in our personal relationships and even more in relations between large and small countries. I was and on this point remain a cynic who doesn't need to be taught this lesson. However, the occasional reminder is salutary.

---

[14] "ball-buster": a translation of *rompicoglioni*, but "pain in the arse" would have been a more idiomatic translation [editor's note].

V

What the Local Historian and the Englishman Had to Say

My next meeting was with Mrs Margaret O'Neill at a large soulless pub with a large car park. It was convenient for parking, she had explained. And she was not wrong. The staff inside were genuinely pleasant and courteous, but this undoubted plus was not enough to remove the odour of a stuffy and synthetic environment. At 11 o'clock in the morning, it was of course almost empty with a lost soul reading a paper in a corner of one of the many compartments which its spaciousness was divided into. The paper was more for companionship than for reading matter, because he stared continuously out of the window, possibly waiting for somebody, and occasionally he would turn a page with barely a glance at it. The silence was not unpleasant, as it seemed appropriate to the deadness of the place.

Then in strode Mrs O'Neill, a huge woman and a huge presence. She had appeared to be insistent on her title, and I was expecting an austere and businesslike woman, and she was businesslike in her own way but not austere. She looked around at me and the man with the paper, and correctly assessed, before I could move, that I was the journalist. Without approaching, she offered me a drink, and after I had pointed to my coffee which was sitting there undrunk and acting as an entrance ticket, she immediately made for the bar and bought herself a pint of dark beer, which she lost no time in clattering down on my table while spilling some of its froth on my notepad.

"Mr Oblivy," she barked with the smile of one who enjoys

life because they cannot think of anything more sensible to do – an attractive quality that by no means signals naivety.

I nodded the affirmative with another smile – this one bemused.

"So what is it you want to know about Kilmarnock, Mr Oblivy?" and she took a swig of her beer.

Even after all these years working as a journalist I often find myself ill-prepared for that question, and usually it's in the presence of someone I feel will judge me – someone who seems to assess people quickly and very possibly accurately. This can be unnerving, so I clung on to the bemused smile, or I thought I did.

"I'm reporting on the referendum, and the question of deindustrialisation often comes up."

"Too right it does. There used to be a lot of mining in the surrounding villages, which has completely disappeared. There was locomotive production ..." and here she leapt into a detailed history of a company that went through many iterations, starting with Andrew Barclay, Sons and Co., and ended up diminished and a subsidiary of an American corporation called Wabtec Rail Scotland, but was still making some locomotives. BMK Carpets had abandoned the town; the shoemaker Saxone and the distillery Johnnie Walker had also closed their doors, whereas the hydraulic engineers Glenfield and Kennedy produced only valves now and were no longer a large employer. And the list went on, and not always concerning the key years of deindustrialisation. Massey Ferguson closed its tractor factory in the seventies.

"And what was the effect on the town?" I asked.

"Devastating. A town becomes a different place when things like that happen. The certainties go from life, and many folk have to get work elsewhere. But there was resistance. The Labour Party moved to the left in the early eighties. The Red Flag flew at the cross, and when the councillors played a charity football match to support the miners, their side dressed fully in red. At the height of the miners' strike, the local communities felt under siege. This is where the independence movement started to take over from the one for devolution. That and the poll tax introduced to Scotland as a test ahead of England with Scotland's voice not heard. The media will tell you that these things made no difference, but this just means that they don't want that to be the case. Have they asked any folk? I doubt it.

"I was campaigning for Yes in Govan a few days ago – that's where they used to build the ships – and I asked a wifie how she was going to vote. She threw me a deafie and I let her go. Mebbie because of that, she turned round and let me have it full blast. She ranted on about Thatcher having thrown her da out of his job, and ruined his life. And she wasnae wrong. Folk don't forget. Only when all the generations have run through, not after two or three decades."[15]

"And was the situation in Kilmarnock typical of the whole of Scotland?"

"Pretty much. At least the Central Belt."

She talked at length about the town and the region, and clearly it was her passion. She told me, for instance, that during the sixties – times of full employment – up to seventy buses would set off for Blackpool when all the factories closed for their summer break. At the end of the journey they would clamber down into the street to meet more of their own neighbours. That was mass society as it must have existed across Europe. Before my time. And it struck me that there's no need to travel in order to have a full and interesting life. All that is in one place is everywhere in differing quantities. There's as much variety in the highly circumscribed as there is in the vast, and what the latter

---

[15] It would appear that the translator has taken it upon himself to reconstruct this character's idiom from supposition; he was after all translating from the Italian and could not have known how she spoke [editor's note].

gains in breadth, it loses in depth. She appeared to work as hard as any academic historian or national journalist, often for nothing and probably always with greater integrity.

At the end of this sometimes difficult conversation to follow – due in part to the vernacular and in part to the abundance of data she provided – I discovered the prickliness so common to small and put-upon nations. I asked a question out of pure curiosity, "Why, if all these things were happening, did the Scots not rebel more fiercely? In the seventies, Italy was awash with protests over much lesser things."

"Who are *you* to judge us?" she asked severely. "Why d'ye think that ye're better than us?"

"What a strange question as a response to my own! If there's one *good* thing about me, it's that I never judge. My parents weren't good, but they never stopped judging. Pointlessly. They got up in the morning, listened to the radio and tut-tutted, and they kept tut-tutting all day long. I'm sure that the last thing they said at night before they fell into the blessed sleep of the righteous was a judgement on politicians, society, the young and God knows what other things they thought they knew about. Theirs was an entirely secular righteousness, but righteousness nevertheless. And yet they did nothing with it. They didn't join political parties, and they didn't go to meetings or demonstrations. Well, maybe the odd demonstration before I was born, from what I understood. They lived in the zeitgeist: left-wing when everyone else was, and then shifting rightwards with the passing years. Without realising it, my father became quite right-wing, and I'm sure that my mother would have too, had she lived.

"That's why I have never judged. Surely it's beyond us. In my philosophy, there is no good and evil, just people struggling incessantly in their own self-interest. Once it seemed heroic, but recently I've started to see it as grubby. And yet incessant, tireless judgement is also grubby, and vain and pointless too.

"Perhaps I'm wrong. Perhaps I simply reacted to my parents. Our parents are gods when we're small, but by the time we're eighteen, they're dull, so very dull. As I say, I've recently rethought this: perhaps all that tut-tutting was heroic, or at least more heroic than the ceaseless, greedy jostling of my own generation."

She smiled: "Quite a speech. I got ye wrong. I thought that ye wanted to judge, when ye didn't even want to know. Ye're just doing yer job, which ye possibly find a drag."

"My job? I don't even know what my job is any more." And I could have added that now I did want to know, and asked myself another question, "Does wanting to know always lead to wanting to judge?"

And in the meantime she had downed a second pint glass of that dark liquid – "liquid bread" as the Czechs call it. And then she was off with barely a nod in my direction. With considerably less verve, I put my things away in my folder and my pockets, and set off for the Dick Institute, Kilmarnock's principal library and example of early twenti-eth-century civic largesse, in search of some books on the subject.

It says a great deal about Scotland in the spring and summer of 2014 that the finest Englishman I ever met I met not in London where I lived for twelve years, but in a town some twenty miles south-west of Glasgow. You can fail to understand the country you were born and brought up in, so it should not come as a surprise that even extended sojourns in other countries only provide partial knowledge. To know anywhere – or anyone for that matter – takes effort. Beyond the hype and bluster of the Unionist politicians, there is a tolerant England, and it's often the case that the finest examples of a virtue are to be found where that virtue is under siege.

I met him in the café at the Dick Institute, a lean man of medium build with a pleasant, handsome face and a shock of blond hair, he introduced himself having heard me talking to one of the librarians.

"An Italian interested in the history of Kilmarnock – that's unexpected."

"Why?"

"Good question. Why not! But I suspect that there is a reason and that's what I'm fishing for."

"I'm a journalist, and don't usually take my job that seriously, but all that I know about Kilmarnock concerns brutal deindustrialisation. I thought that I should ..."

"... mug up on it, you mean. That makes sense. You've satisfied my curiosity."

"Are you from here?" I asked, knowing that he wasn't, and as curious about him as he had been about me.

"No, no," he smiled, "I'm from London. Yesterday I was giving a talk in Glasgow, one of my favourite cities. There I heard that a Scottish politician I admire would be giving a speech here in Kilmarnock tonight. I decided to stay over and return home tomorrow."

"You mean Jim Paterson. I'll be there myself."

"Really?" his interest reawakening. "How did you hear of him?"

"I have someone advising me. Actually he doesn't approve of Paterson."

"Ah, why would that be?"

"Paterson left Labour long ago, and campaigns for independence. My adviser – he's called George – believes that I'm now safe enough to be exposed to dangerous ideas," I laughed as I said it.

"And are you?"

"I'm not here to take sides," I said more seriously, uncertain not only of who I was talking to but also of my own feelings.

"But you will," he said with a smile.

"I don't think so. It's not my job and it's not my country."

"Of course it's not your job, but you're a human being,

aren't you? Are you only interested in your own country? Blinkered for anyone, I would say, but fatal for a journalist, however news-weary and disengaged."

"Why this one?"

"Because every issue here concerns us all in Europe: nation, wealth distribution, globalisation, the deindustrialisation you mentioned, and of course migration, on which the Scots have an extraordinarily progressive approach – not all but many, that is many more than in England and some other parts of Europe. For once we have a referendum that has some intellectual clout, and it is surprisingly under-reported, particularly in England."

"And yet you're English?"

"Very much so."

"English English through and through?"

"Well, yes and no. Not so much on my mother's side, though she was brought up in England from the age of nine. She was half Italian and half Austrian."

"Let's hear about it, then."

"As long as you don't write about it in your newspaper! My grandfather was a rural policeman in Austria, and had fought in the First World War as a very young man. My grandmother was a maid from Belluno and was in service at the castle of a rich Jewish industrialist. Until she married my grandfather in 1934 she also worked in Vienna where his main residence was. It wasn't a bad life until the Anschluss, which upset the industrialist who was married to a gentile and whose sons bizarrely became active Nazis. The atmosphere was so poisoned after Hitler extended his power to Austria that he could never feel at ease. On one occasion he left Vienna for his castle to have some rest from the fevered madness of those years, and as soon as he arrived, the local Nazis, conscious of his arrival, improvised a military parade complete with jingoistic music in the square below. This shattered his calm and everyone had to return to Vienna. All his entourage – governesses and maids included – were unpacking their bags and had to repack them hurriedly. He left for Argentina shortly after the start of the war, but never got over his fright. He died within a year of fleeing his homeland – and was also collateral damage forgotten in the maelstrom of death.

"Things got more difficult for my mother's family. When Yugoslavia was invaded, my grandfather was posted to Bosnia. He was still a policeman, but one in a foreign land whose language he didn't know. One day when patrolling alone on his military motorbike, he was shot by a partisan. His body was never returned.

"My grandmother left for Belluno, leaving my mother and uncle – two years older than she was – with relations of my grandfather. The idea was to send for them when she was in a position to look after them. She never was.

"The war ended and my mother and uncle ended up in a camp for displaced civilians in Switzerland. This was not a bad experience – they were well looked-after by the standards of the ruined continent. In 1946, the Red Cross incredibly traced my grandmother not to Belluno, but to London where she had gone to work and had married an Englishman.

"This was not a happy ending. Their stepfather was a xenophobe in spite of his choice of wife, and much later would become a member of the National Front. My grandmother had two more children whose names I do not even know, and my mother and uncle grew up at the periphery of that family. Both were damaged. More so my uncle who lived out his life alone in a tiny bedsit in the Guinness Building in Hammersmith and mostly worked as a delivery driver for a small family firm – a gentle man who always kept a dog and cared more about animals than human beings. The only person he trusted was my mother, and perhaps the only person she loved was him. He had looked after her when they were homeless, and the strain of that responsibility when still so young had possibly been too much for him.

I often visited the Guinness Building, which resembled a prison with a central cavity within the walkways that provided the entrances to the cell-like flats. It was a limbo in which the semi-destitute lived, and though grey with tiredness, the residents or perhaps I should call them inmates always seemed kindly and polite. There existed a camaraderie of the defeated, but my uncle held aloof even from them. He was alone where the sounds and smells of human company were never far away.

"When my mother and uncle were teenagers, they cut all relations with their family and struck out on their own. My mother worked hard and was ambitious, but it was her marriage that changed her life. My uncle had always kept his German, and spoke it to his sister and mother, though not in the presence of his stepfather as this could cause even more violence to be inflicted on him. He always kept a slight trace of a German accent; perhaps he actually held on to it, but as far as I know he never travelled outside England for the rest of his life. One of my mother's many activities was to teach German at evening classes, and it was there that she met my father, a stockbroker in the city.

"My grandmother got back in touch with my family after my step-grandfather died. She seemed to have lost all contact with her children of that family, and my uncle would never talk to her. My mother was different. She insisted on accepting her, in spite of some reticence from my father. Four decades after the war, it was still difficult for our family to come together, and in fact it never did. And all this was the direct consequence of one partisan squeezing the trigger of what was probably an outdated rifle. I don't blame him, as my grandfather was in his country with powers to order the local police around – those who had agreed to collaborate. He came as the invader and the victor, even though he may not have wanted to go. Refusal was barely an option, and not an option for a man wanting a quiet life, in as much as a quiet life was possible in those times.

Perhaps the partisan was sweating at the time, terrified of what would happen if he failed to kill the enemy who was undoubtedly armed with the latest machine gun. Maybe he wasn't even part of an organised group, but a hunter who had hid in the roadside wood when he heard a motorbike coming. Maybe it was a spontaneous act, an anonymous protest against these foreigners who had turned his world upside down. Maybe he was a farmer or even a doctor or teacher who returned home and never spoke of it to anyone for the rest of his life, but the following morning, his hand shook when he started to shave and every time he saw a German soldier, fear grasped his entrails and squeezed them pitilessly. He cannot be blamed; indeed, I would say that he acted with courage against a mighty and ruthless enemy.

"But nor was my grandfather to blame, I think. He was a victim too. When my grandmother came to live with our family late in her life, she refused to speak of her recently dead husband or her children by him, but she did give us our first information about my grandfather. He was never a Nazi, she said, and he had no choice but to accept the posting in Yugoslavia. It was either that or a soldier at the front – in Russia perhaps. In other words, where his chances of survival would have been diminished further. He may not have hated Jews or Gypsies, but he almost certainly did not speak up against the criminal manner in which they were treated.

"Of course, she may not have been a reliable witness, and who knows how well she knew her husband's thoughts? If she knew them well, it would have been a good but unusual marriage. He remains a cipher, and perhaps represents those millions who were dragged into acts and decisions they were incapable of measuring up to. If he was not entirely innocent, innocent were those who would suffer after he fell from his motorbike fatally wounded. And that was just one man. Multiply him by millions across this continent and try to tell me that war is not an obscenity and we needn't do all we can to avoid another!"

"I wouldn't try, partly because I was already persuaded," I replied, a little stunned by the story and its not so hidden rhetoric, but also fascinated. "So you're not really English at all."

"Oh, I am, I can assure you," he continued without pause, "on my father's side I was. English and middle class. You could say that I'm the quintessential Englishman: not because I'm representative of how the majority of the English think, but because I'm representative of what most English people are. My background is both working class and middle class, both immigrant and native, and both European and Little English. If I had a sex change, I could run in the competition for the most English person in the world, and yet I'm an untypical Englishman precisely because I'm representative of the whole."

"So on your father's side, you're completely English?"

"As far as we know, but there never were any pure Anglo-Saxons, or pure anything anywhere. There has always been migration, but until the discovery of America it was continental, and then with a flourish of Columbus's deadly wand, it was global. And it really was deadly for the non-Europeans, though in America they got their own back with a bit of syphilis and in Africa with malaria. In recent times, global migration has gone back up to nineteenth-century levels but the directions of travel have changed. No one but the pure-blooded worries about this. And of course pure-bloodedness is a myth – always a myth. Nowhere can it exist, not even in remote communities, where you'll find a higher degree of miscegenation than they would normally be willing to admit.

"But myths must be solid things, if they can cause wars and massacres. A Nazi may believe himself to be a pure Teuton, and an Israeli may believe himself to be a pure Jew, but the pure Teuton may be less Teutonic than an Ashkenazi Jew and the Israeli will almost definitely have less DNA of the original Israelites than a Palestinian. Of course both Germany and Israel-Palestine are on thoroughfares, and people have been either marching or traipsing through both of them since prehistory."

"These are statements that could offend and could easily be misunderstood."

"Of course, people don't like you to meddle with their myths."

"But people don't invent their pedigrees, do they? And if you can go back six or seven generations, that should be enough, surely?"

"I'm reminded of a series of long arguments I had with a Londoner abroad on holiday. We met on several occasions, and he was nice man – a little prickly perhaps, but life had not been treating him well. And we always argued over immigration. He wasn't a racist, but he was fiercely anti-immigrant. I know that the distinction is not a clear-cut one, and often people who are racist don't like the label. On the third or fourth time I met him, he revealed something that I found impossible to understand: he said, as though it were of little relevance, 'You do realise that my parents were Greek. I was born in London, but they came from Greece.' I must have been visibly shocked; I couldn't get my head round it. Of course, he justified this with those specious arguments such people use. His parents were a different generation of immigrants. They came to work, and all that nonsense.

"So I don't really care. Of course, we're all a mixture but even when our family history should take us in the direction of complete tolerance, we can, if we so wish, create our own personal myths to justify intolerance."

"But he's right, these are different generations."

"Of course generations are very different. But I see no evidence that this generation of immigrants wants to work less than previous ones – quite the opposite."

"But generations are different from each other," I said, and could not help thinking of the gulf there had always been between me and my parents.

"Of course. I would never deny that. The other day as I left work in the early evening, I noticed a young couple. Joined loosely by the hands, they bounced up steps leading to a side street, both painfully thin. It appeared, however, that they didn't feel any pain about themselves or their place in life. Indeed, they were clearly full of hope and perhaps even happiness, something I could never associate with my own youth and childhood. This pleased me. No one had raised a rod to this new generation and this had freed them from the prison walls of imposed behaviour. Quite possibly the way they had been solicitously organised and deferred to in childhood had created another kind of prison wall. Quite possibly every generation has a wall to tear down. Quite possibly every generation should have a wall to tear down. How else can they know who they are? How else can they find something to do with their lives?"

"No one raised a rod to me."

"You're Italian and quite a bit younger than me. Things have changed for the better. I went to a military establishment, so I probably got the worst schooling of my generation, but for everyone in my generation, physical violence was to some extent a part of their education."

"A military establishment?"

"Yes, my father came from a long line of military men. He broke that continuum and wanted me to resume it. His choice of school had the opposite effect. Besides, my mother who had suffered so much as a child because of the war told me plenty of stories that didn't encourage bellicose dreaming."

"So if you're English, what have the Scots to complain about?"

"They have a lot to complain about, but England – like Scotland, like anywhere – is something much more complex than anything that can be expressed in a TV vox pop. Commentators and politicians repeat incessantly that the British or the English are a tolerant and fair-minded people.

They're not wrong, but they're not right either. England is not a particularly tolerant nation, and your country, Italy, is – or at least the balance is more in favour of tolerance – but I have never heard anyone in Italy say that theirs is a tolerant country. With exceptions of course, they just do it. I have travelled extensively in Italy and Austria, and I wouldn't say that Austria is particularly tolerant, but tolerance exists, as it does everywhere. Ultimately tolerance is a personal moral choice.

"Where there have been empires recently, as in France and Britain, it's often difficult to be self-aware. What Scotland has done is that it has come up with this wonderful but quite simple idea: a national community based on residence and not on blood and land. Originally people defined their nationality by blood alone. The nations were often mixed up together, and when they moved, as they often did, the nation moved with them. Then the nation became a territory owned by blood, which as I have said is a mythical and abstract concept. And now the Scots are saying that it's a territory owned by whoever comes and disowned by everyone who leaves. It is a culture. It is a culture that people can take up or abandon. So it's a modern concept, a new concept and it could well be the future. A victory for independence in the Scottish referendum would be a victory for this concept and therefore for humanity, and a new model of citizenship. And that's why I'm here.

"Of course, it wouldn't be the first time if the Scottish nation did not fulfil all its promises, because political and social realities are much more viscous than they may first appear. Huge changes can occur in societies, but periods of change often lead to periods of reversal, and the only changes that stick are the changes that enter into our minds. That's not easy. But still, particularly when I go to events such as the one we'll be at this evening, I feel that big changes for a small country are on their way, and because we're neighbours we too will start to change – eventually."

"So what were you giving a talk on yesterday evening?"

"Frederick II. I'm a historian, and I specialise in the history of the Holy Roman Empire."

"You're an academic?"

"Yes. Does that surprise you?"

"Yes, and the subject surprises me in someone so wrapped up in their own times. I also find that academics have become so insular, so restricted to small subject areas. As though anything can be understood without context. I preferred to go into journalism, because it's all context and no specialism. It may appear shallow, and often is, but in some way – however distorted – it communicates the world to itself."

"I couldn't agree more. I study my own subject of course because I want to know about it in itself, but it also tells me a great deal about my own times. It was one of the many attempts to unite Europe, and like them all it had weaknesses. It's an unusual subject in that it covers a millennium, from its inception with the Empire of Charlemagne to its demise in the late-eighteenth century at the hands of another attempt to unite Europe: Napoleon's more short-lived one. With a subject like that, context is everything, but you're right, no subject can be entirely isolated from its temporal and geographic context in the humanities or from its adjacent disciplines in science."

"So what drove you to the Holy Roman Empire?"

"Can't you guess? I have Austrian and Italian roots, and like my mother and my siblings, I speak German perfectly. I also speak passable Italian, though not as good as your excellent English. When he was Home Secretary, David Blunkett said that immigrants should only speak English, even at home. We'll leave aside the idiocy of this remark, but I would argue the opposite: another language helps me to be English; it in no way undermines my Englishness. To relate this to what we've just been talking about, English is my specialism and German is my context. It could be any other European language. Another language allows you to view yourself through other people's eyes. Obviously it also helps you to be a European."

He was right: by living abroad in Europe, I had become a European. It's not that difficult; we all share many of the same virtues and vices. And a few days earlier, I had learnt that I had lost contact with the great majority of Europeans, even the ones living in my own country. In other words, I had been a national European, and living abroad turned me into a cosmopolitan European, but the real European rooted both in a particular place, who nevertheless primarily identifies with Europe, that is something yet to come. Such people exist, but not yet enough to save Europe should some political tempest hit our accident-prone continent.

When I went to Paterson's Yes rally, I was looking around to see if I would find my friend – the representative Englishman – and that was the better part of me, because I knew that I could learn from him. In fact, I would meet someone who would teach me much more than I would ever have expected, though not until after the event. In Scotland the question and answer sessions can go on for a long time, and when they end most of the public rush off, a few stopping to buy a publication or have a chat at the exit. My guess is that most of those go straight home, whereas the activists who move around between one event and another usually have no home to go to, so naturally they wander off for a drink and some food. I was of course of their number, though different as very few journalists, even Scottish ones, went to such events. So when I went into a pub, I recognised some of the activists and one in particular, as we'd exchanged a few words in Glasgow.

On seeing her I decided not to order food, in spite of my hunger, but to quickly acquire a half pint of beer and get to the empty chair next to her before anyone else did. The group was already quite loud, as was the piped music, but this is more or less standard. I dropped into the seat and turning said with feigned surprise, "Hello, remember me?"

"Not really," she replied, barely adjusting in her seat, "should I?"

She had a good head of dark black hair that came down just below the back of the neck, and regular features. But her face was animated by a kind of intellectual determination that meant she had to study every eventuality carefully before she decided on what action to take. The overall effect was far from welcoming, but I found it attractive, and it was an attraction I failed to control.

"I would expect you to, because you told me to fuck off," I answered, and someone laughed.

"You must have been really irritating, so why would I want to remember that?"

"I was, so let me apologise," I had decided to be submissive. I thought this a clever ploy, but it would colour my behaviour throughout our relationship.

"Apology accepted, now get lost!"

"Come on, Maryanne, give the guy a chance. He's just apologised," one of the women said, and then she turned to me. "Where are you from?"

"Italy."

"Really, where in Italy?"

"Lugo di Romagna, but you won't have heard of it."

"No, I can't say that have, but it sounds fantastic. Is it perched on a hill covered with cypress trees?"

"No, it's in the plain, and it's a manufacturing town, or at least it was."

"A bit like Kilmarnock; it used to make everything and now it makes nothing. How do they manage?"

"I don't know. It seems wealthier than it was back then, but there are still some factories left."

"Well, that's something. There's not much here."

The conversation was of the wrong kind and with the wrong person, but this was not the moment for bad manners. I tried instead to change its course: "To be honest, I haven't been back to my home town for twelve years; in fact I haven't even been to Italy in that time. I don't know that much more than you do."

"You must ring home now and then."

"Not really. My father does ring occasionally."

"You're not married then?" said Maryanne. "You have that married look about you. Don't you think, Jenny? Definitely lying in my book." And she turned away again.

"Separated," I said, and although this word was never mentioned by me or my wife, it could, after twelve years of not seeing each other, be reasonably defined as a separation.

"Why is it that I find it very difficult to believe a word you say?" Maryanne joined in again.

"Maybe you just don't like foreigners," I smiled.

"Good try, but it's not that. You could be from down the road and it'd make no difference. If you want to know, it's yer dial[16] that's got lying toerag written all over it. I'm not saying I don't believe that you're separated. That I can believe, but it's your whole manner – the way you look at me."

"Come on, Maryanne, he's not that bad. You hardly know him."

"I don't want to. He was trying to smooth up to me the other night, and I told him to fuck off then and I'm making it clear now, and still he doesn't get the message."

---

[16] "yer dial": English in the original, and Cinico provided an explanation, which I will translate back into English for the benefit of most anglophone readers – "This term is used in Glasgow and some other parts of Scotland to mean 'your face' [translator's note]." This was one of De Oblivii's two notes, but Cameron spoke on one occasion of the author's considerable difficulty in understanding the Scottish vernacular, particularly in the western Central Belt, and this to some extent justifies Cameron's attempt to reconstruct the likely register without knowing exactly how it would have been [editor's note].

My dignity could take no more, though I did think of persevering. I stood up and said, "I've got it now, and I'll be going."

"You're welcome to stay," Jenny said, "You don't have to talk to her. She often goes off on one. It's just her nature."

"No, thank you, you're very kind, but I had better be going. I've got to see some people tomorrow morning and then I'll be travelling to Inverness in the afternoon."

And as I turned to leave, I heard Maryanne under her breath: "Good riddance!" The English language, which can occasionally fail to satisfy when it comes to heated argument, is the supreme instrument for dismissiveness. The quietness was all the more effective for coming from a forthright woman, and the knife could not have gone deeper.

VI

What the Frenchwoman and the
Dying Man Had to Say

It seems to me that in Western society everything is now ruled by the gregarious. In any walk of life, the self-confident purveyors of platitudes are at conferences, industry events complete with mutual compliments and prizes, seminars, network sessions and the like, and they re-establish almost on a daily basis their conquest of power, but have little time to implement even the delivery of a paper clip. Saner people avoid these gatherings as they would an infectious disease, and the careers of saner people are dead. For an Italian this is strange, as we're not so enamoured of what the British call "small talk". However, I take great pleasure in observing these people as they work the floor, exchanging and dispensing the grotesquely insincere. Not that insincerity is unknown in Italy; far from it, we probably invented it, but we deliver it to potentates whose identity is clearly established: our country is a mosaic of principalities. Whether a factory, firm, province or township, there is always a prince to whom the wise should pay court. These duties can be carried out summarily and then we return to the more gratifying business of being ourselves. We know how to divide off the world of work from the world of home and friends. I don't care a damn which is the more democratic. Neither, I suspect.

In my opinion, the British are more restrained than Americans in their flattery, and more generous with it than Europeans. Of the British, Scots are more European and measure the doses more carefully. I speak of the middle classes; the Scottish working class, as I observed over the campaign, has a laudable distrust of flattery, while the middle class is more integrated in the British and indeed global Anglo-Saxon culture. As always the situation is more complex because some sections of the middle class are the most consciously Scottish element of Scottish society, for instance parts of the legal professions, the media and the "cultural industries". No doubt the British establishment has realised this, and at this very moment some Whitehall bureaucrats are discussing how these elements can be infiltrated, marginalised or bought off. Fulfil their careers and they'll forget all radical fervour. Or perhaps the British establishment has lost its touch, and relies now solely on bluster and fear.

So when I found myself in Inverness with yet another group of doctors, lawyers, businesspeople, local politicians and the odd writer or actor all queuing up for their free glass of wine as if it were their human right, I wasn't at all fazed by the inane conversation and brazen flattery. Of course, George had arranged our invites and as we came along in the taxi, I didn't even bother to ask him what it was about. It had New Labour stamped all over it, and New Labour differs from Thatcherism only in the sense that its adherents feel that they're all very moral. They're the ones who care, apparently. And equally unremarkable was the fact they were No voters to a man, but in a corner I noticed a woman who most certainly wasn't.

I looked across at her and she smiled. It must be hard for those who do not know how to switch on a smile. Their hearts could be much more genuine than mine – it would not be difficult – but somehow their shyness prevents them from expressing those feelings. They are dumb in the language of emotion, but emotion boils inside them where it's trapped. Maryanne and I did not suffer from that problem: her smile was a signal to me, and my anger – for anger it was, I'm afraid – immediately dissolved and my own smile wished to reply, but I suppressed it until I was just a few seconds away from her to make it more effective. "What are you doing in place like this? Not your scene I would have thought," I asked as I decided to shake her hand at this stage, rather than embrace her.

"Was I a complete bastard last night?" she exchanged my question with another, and her evasiveness made me in my narcissism think that she had found out where I was going and got there before me. After all, she knew I was going to Inverness.

"And was I a complete bastard the night before last?"

"Yes, I can confirm that you were, but that's no excuse for me to …," she smiled again instead of ending the sentence.

"Then we have both paid our debts to boorishness, and I was the one who started it," I was enjoying being gallant, though it wasn't in my nature. Just this once.

She put her arm through mine and dragged me to the door, "Let's get out of here, the place is hoachin' not just with No voters, but with bigwig No voters. I'll get myself into trouble if I hang about much longer. Just listen to them!" And I put up no resistance.

As we had abandoned a free buffet, we made our way to a small restaurant. She commanded and I followed. For a moment I couldn't understand why I had always thought this a bad idea. Letting stuff happen to you is both adventurous and a great deal less effort. When you've eaten out as much as I have, the whole scene becomes very dull, from the overly thought-out decor to the solicitous waiter who accompanies you to your seat. Why would I want to decide, when actually I no longer cared.

As soon as we had ordered, Maryanne was talking politics and occasionally she asked my opinion. I answered in the manner I thought she wanted to hear, while I continued to study and enjoy her physical presence and her mannerisms. I was of course unpractised in the arguments in favour of the Yes vote, and I noted that she had never asked me that fatal question – how would I vote if I had the vote – because I had told her that I didn't have one, still being a resident in London, and my vote was not to be won by either side. She possibly didn't ask it because she was afraid of what the answer might be.

Quite suddenly she stood up and ran to the door. At first this action by someone so unpredictable disturbed me but then I saw her remonstrating with the waiter who apparently was turning away a woman of around fifty years with slightly greying hair, the restaurant now being entirely full. She then returned with the woman whom she introduced as Cécile. "She'll be dining with us," she proclaimed.

Ours was a table for four, and the waiter had removed the two extra places. Now he had to reinstate one of them, and he did so with measured resentment. He was perhaps a man who disliked the unexpected and the unusual. If Maryanne detected that resentment, she showed no sign of it. She was absorbed with making the Frenchwoman feel at ease, and asked a number of questions about her life and why she was visiting Inverness. But inevitably, it was stronger than her very considerable will, and she had to talk about the referendum. She tried to explain about why Scotland needed to do this: deindustrialisation, the poll tax, the persistent English vice of electing Conservative governments and the Scots' equal persistence in voting against them. But she didn't find fertile ground.

"I like the English – the Scottish too, of course," said the Frenchwoman.

"I would think so," Maryanne responded sternly, "There's the Auld Alliance!"

"What is the Auld Alliance?"

"You haven't heard of it? The French and the Scots were really close once."

"So were many countries that later went to war with each other. I think that the Scottish finished off our Napoleon at Waterloo. He nearly won, and the Prussians were late. Just imagine: if it weren't for you, Europe would have been united a long time ago and probably no world wars in the last century. Still I don't hold it against you," she smiled. "And I have to say that I like the English."

Maryanne, who was by no means anti-English, was a little flustered that she couldn't get Cécile to understand the political situation. "Oh yeah, and they call you 'cheese-eating surrender monkeys'."

"Of course I know this, said by a Scotsman in an American cartoon, but the English really, how do you say, ran with the ball. This is just part of their charm, don't you think?"

"Not really!"

Cécile raised an eyebrow and allowed herself a suppressed smile, "I didn't say that I want to be English. We know very well how to live in France, but I wouldn't want the English to become French: it would be so dull. You see, the English xenophobia is so egalitarian because it affects everyone else on the planet, even their fellow Anglo-Saxons across the ocean. They are wonderfully indiscriminate. And their sense of humour is very amusing, though not exactly in the way they intend. I like their innate certitude that they are the best nation in the world and that everyone else secretly agrees with them about this. We're a bit like that in France, or we used to be. It comes with empire, you know. It's silly, but also charming in a way. You Scots should be careful that you don't gain a nation and lose a sense of humour. It's not that your hands are entirely clean either."

By now Maryanne was smiling, and to show no ill will she filled the Frenchwoman's wine glass close to the brim. "There's no danger of that," she said, "but this is a crucial moment in my country's history. There are times when things go beyond humour, as they govern nearly all your days and all your actions."

"It is precisely in moments like these that it is so important. Humour humanises ..."

"… and dehumanises, as with racist jokes. Humour blurs reason."

"You are correct," the Frenchwoman conceded, "humour also dehumanises, but I have in my head this idea of humanising humour that brings us back together and, how do you say, becalms the agitations."

After an evening in the bar and having parted company with Cécile, we walked along the Ness in silence for a bit – at a loss and uncertain about the next step. She stopped and turned to me, and I knew then that she had made up her mind: "Cinico, you've probably guessed that I came to Inverness to see you. Actually I found you attractive the minute I saw you, which is why I found your arsey behaviour so irritating. But when you left last night, I decided that I had to find out who you really are, so I knew you were going to Inverness and only had to look up whatever moronic events your professor was likely to have arranged, and I got it in one. Not so much goes on in Inverness.

"I should also say that you should change the company you keep. It's not good for you.

"And another thing: you don't get to sleep with me this evening. I've still got to think it over. When I'm ready I'll tell you."

I was restored to my normal narcissistic self, which had been acute in its assessment of her motives. Her insistence on having me wait I accepted with equanimity, as things were moving faster than I could have imagined. I thanked her, I kissed her, I smiled and I turned to leave. After barely twenty-five metres, she shouted my name and when I turned, she indicated with her head that I should follow her. I ran after her and she was already crossing one of the bridges. When I caught up, she said, "This isn't going to look good. I only dropped off my bag a few hours ago. These people don't know me. Still, who cares?"

I had nothing to add. At the door of a small cottage

on two floors, she produced a key and we entered a corridor stuffed with placards and leaflets scattered carelessly across the floor. From the front room I could hear heated conversation and raucous laughter. We didn't look in, but climbed the stairs to her room. She seemed to have thought it all out, and immediately placed a chair under the door handle. Without another word she started to undress me, and once we started making love, she insisted on being on top. However, she was a thoughtful lover and appeared to enjoy it. I looked up and she was a magnificent beast who rose above the terrible contingencies of the lives of us lesser animals. A century or two ago, she would have leapt to the barricade armed solely with a flag, and got herself shot no doubt. Perhaps not. Perhaps such people are marked out by history as invulnerable. Garibaldi rode into battle on a white horse, wearing a gaucho's hat and poncho, his head held high and his reddish-blond hair and beard flowing in the wind. All around his comrades were mown down, but he sat astride his mare fully two metres above the others and enjoyed those happiest moments of his life. How many men and women did he draw behind him on his quests? Many of whom were better than he, and they, mere mortals, had to compete with him. For me, the righteousness of her cause counted for little. I was fixated with the symbol and not with the idea it was supposed to represent.

And when it was done, she sank down on to my chest, her warmth smooth and touching in every sense. A closeness she expressed by lying there silently for at least five minutes, and then she rose and told me to get up and dressed. "Not all night for the moment," she said, but it was clear that she wanted to join the debate below. This was a campaign that developed by the hour, and I was a sideshow, though I had no thought of that at the time. I slipped out of the house a happy man.

The following morning the good professor came into

breakfast late, and I saw immediately that he was agitated. I was in a supremely good mood, and this of course was love, but I had not recognised the symptoms, which was understandable in the circumstances: I had never been in love before, and so mine was the love of an eighteen-year-old in spite of my forty years. Given that sexual love often brings with it brotherly love, particularly in its headier moments, I raised my hand to wave and shouted his name. The second he saw me, he hurried across with a large, needy grin on his face. This was disconcerting, but he was about to find me one of the most satisfactory interviews he arranged. I realised then that there was no thought in anything he did: everything around him was erratic but delivered with unchallengeable aplomb, which could be entertaining or, as in this case, instructive and humbling – a moment of exquisite sadness.

"Cinico, something's turned up and you've got to help me out," he panted in his agitation. "An old friend is poorly. Very poorly, to tell the truth. I'm supposed to go and see him – a charming man. I suddenly thought, Cinico would really love to meet him, you'll have so much in common. Of course, he'll be disappointed that I can't make it, but you can make up for that. Tell him I'm on business," he paused, "charity business."

"Poorly, you say. How poorly? Are we talking about deathbed poorly?"

"Well, nobody knows, of course, but he could die. It is serious."

"Come off it, George, you're sending me to the bedside of your dying friend whom I've never seen in my life. Are you mad?"

He looked a little troubled as he searched around his brain for a rational justification. "He could die, but we all could die. He may be more likely to die in the next forty-eight hours than, say, we are, but he's tough and I'm sure he'll pull through."

"You're not convincing me."

He took a different tack; he tried to make me feel guilty. "Listen, Cinico, you owe me this one. I've been working my socks off to get you interviews and information. I'm in a hole, and I'm only asking for a little slack."

"But my paper pays you for doing this, and these days that's lucky, I can tell you."

"Not enough, Cinico, not enough, and of course I always give everything a hundred and ten per cent effort. That's always been my weakness."

In my current and temporary love-induced state of believing the world to be the best of all possible worlds, the idea of dampening my new-found optimism was wholly unattractive, but there's no point in arguing with some people, and the bizarreness of the request almost made me curious – made me want to go, even when my reason was telling me that I would be insane. "Okay, I'll do it, but I don't see the point. You can't send a proxy for this kind of a thing. You don't want to make new acquaintances when you're about to croak; you want to be with your family and friends. If he's you're friend, you should go whatever the discomfort."

"I got a call from his widow."

"Widow?"

"I mean wife. You see what a jitter I'm in."

"That Freudian slip says it all. The man is at his last gasp. I really shouldn't go."

"You've already promised. By the way, where were you last night?"

The drab hospice smelt of old age and old carpets. The nurse, brisk and kindly, appeared to expect me and whisked me away down through corridors that concealed the dying on an industrial scale, to a room where the good professor's dying friend lay. "You have a visitor!" she announced, as she must have spent most of her working day announcing.

The dying man didn't move. I thought perhaps that he was already dead, and stood there waiting – uncomfortable and a little distressed. Eventually he spoke but without raising his head or even moving it at all. "You can sit down, you know. There's a chair for you. Sister put it out this morning."

I sat down and said apologetically – but not as apologetic as I would have liked it to sound, "I'm afraid that George Lovenight couldn't come because of pressing business – charity work, you know. I hope …"

"Thank God for that. The last thing I need in my dying moments is a visit from that bore."

"I thought that George was your friend – that he was well thought of."

"He's a foreigner to you. It's difficult enough to know our own people, let alone foreigners. Don't get me wrong, I love foreigners, precisely because there's always something enigmatic about them. Racists say 'inscrutable', which suggests that foreigners are purposefully or even maliciously hiding something, when in fact they're just being themselves and we don't know how to read the signals. You may think that George is urbane, witty, knowledgeable or whatever you attribute to him, but I can assure you that he's not. George is a bore of Olympian proportions, and is well known for it." Throughout our brief but memorable acquaintance the dying man never moved his head but spoke as though to the ceiling. I doubt that he ever saw my face, but he listened to my presence in the room.

"Let me introduce myself. I'm Cinico de Oblivii, an Italian journalist, and I'm working with George on this referendum."

"De Oblivii, splendid name. I hope you're a writer."

"No, a journalist."

"I was a writer."

"Really, what sort of things did you write?"

"Novels, a bit of poetry, the odd bit of non-fiction. Never

went very far. Difficult to know what it was all about, but it seemed important at the time." He paused: "So you're writing about our referendum?"

"That's correct. I'm writing for my newspaper."

"Well, I'm for it. I really want independence to happen. In fact, I just want to live until we get the result. I know that I'm going to die, but I would like to live a few more months … just make it to the 18th of September or rather the result on the 19th. Not a lot to ask."

"So you're a nationalist?" I asked with perhaps a little disapproval in my voice.

"Not really. If things were like they were when I was born – that was in 1950 – then I would have been against it. In those days, Scotland was badly divided by sectarianism and an outside force to keep that particular cancer under control was a good thing, but now it's a matter of political culture. We have a good one, and at the moment it is England that doesn't, so clearly we need to get independence to realise our beliefs while they still survive. We need it now, and not in twenty years, just as we needed devolution in 1979 and not in 1997. Always too late. Too little, too late."

For me this was a novel argument, and it silenced me. After a long pause, he was the one who started to speak: "It's very good to have another writer visit me when I'm dying."

"I'm not really a writer, I'm a journalist. I'm not even one of those fancy journalists who write columns of fine prose and comment. I'm a hack. For me it's a job, not a calling or vocation."

"If I were to give a young writer some advice …"

"I'm not a writer; I'm a journalist."

Ignoring me he continued, "Just two things really: first I would say, learn a language. Another language tells you so much about your own – its merits and its deficiencies. And about syntax – how you construct a sentence. You should do it anew every time, rather than follow a restrictive template scattered with clichés. That's anathema to a writer."

"And our stock in trade – for a journalist, I mean – we don't have the luxury of time to tweak and play with words. It's where we show our brilliance, the speed of our thought. It's clever too, and fortunately for me we live in a journalistic age – a culture of the minute and the nanosecond, and not of the decade, the century and, far enough back, eternity."

"You may be right, though I've heard that the newspapers are dying. And the second – that's the second thing I'd tell a young writer like you: Be yourself!"

"Ah!" I said.

"Not be yourself in the just-express-yourself-as-the-ideas-pop-into-your-head manner, but as your craft and study dictate to you. Write to please, of course, but don't write to please anyone in particular: the powerful, the critics, fashion, the readers who liked some other writer, because those other writers will be much better at being themselves than you will ever be at being them. I suppose I am saying, 'Be honest, be truthful.' If this whole business of literature is worth anything – and that's a big if – then it has to seek the truth. Small truths, I think, because big truths evade most of us."

He lay quietly on his bed for a while, tired by his rant. He smiled and muttered, "I talk too much, you must forgive me."

I was now completely lost for words, which is unusual.

After another long pause he said, evidencing the direction his thoughts had gone in the meantime, "I'm not afraid to die, you know. Part of me died long ago."

He paused again, but this time it felt as though he were on the brink of saying something he wasn't entirely sure that he should say. Immediately the curiosity of a professional journalist came to the fore, however world-weary I may have felt. I needed to know and was direct, "What do you mean, part of you died long ago?"

He paused again, clearly questioning his own motivations and proprieties. "My daughter was raped. What made it worse was that the culprit was a young artist I befriended. Not so much an artist as a wealthy and indolent rake who needed a title to justify his place in this world. I never saw any of his work, if in fact it existed."

"And your daughter blamed you?"

"I don't think so. She never said anything to suggest that. I blamed myself though. I couldn't have known – or could I, if I were a better judge of character? Families are governed by silences, not just because bad things are done in families, but also because in the best of families we are one, and the wounds affect everyone. We remain silent, each tending to our own wounds. We have no choice: to talk about it would mean opening out the wounds further. The talking cure is a myth."

"I'm not sure about that, but it's certainly not Northern European."

"I suppose you're right. You do it differently in Mediterranean Europe. And perhaps the thing is that we should respect our own cultures and customs. What works for you, doesn't work for us."

"And yet you've told me."

"You're a fellow writer and an Italian – and you'll go back to Italy. I'm about to die and even the stiffest upper lip is entitled to quiver at a moment like this."

"So you *are* a little fearful of death?" I asked, doubtful of an honest answer.

"Not at all," he flashed back with the hint of a smile directed at the ceiling. "I think that it's not-living that people should be frightened of – not living in the moment and savouring it. People come up against evil or, call it what you want, psychopathic behaviour. Evil is an old-fashioned term used inappropriately by American presidents, but it has the merit of being a catch-all. When people do encounter it, their psyche is damaged. If someone looses a leg in battle, it shows, but damage to the psyche is hidden and it too can never be wholly cured. But living with physical or psychological damage does not mean that parts of you are not very much alive; it doesn't mean that there are no more moments of joy, if you can learn from the experience. The real living dead are those who follow the behaviour patterns many consider the ideal in our Western societies: the ruthless pursuit of our own economic self-interest. They are like the overbred cattle that graze on the hillside, but worse, because all that manic pursuit of comfort and consumption results in untold damage to this planet."

I thought for a moment that perhaps the most important thing we do in life is conversation, particularly conversations that feel unscripted – conversations that take us by surprise.

"Leaving aside the referendum – an entirely contingent matter, my worry is not how much I linger in this world, which for me is the only one, but I would like to leave it in the certainty that human beings are fundamentally good and not programmable through economic incentive. If Milton Friedman was right to think that we're always motivated by economic self-interest, it would be better to have a planet of robots or a planet empty of everything, like Mars. Of course he's wrong, but he's not completely wrong now. A culture of economic fragmentation is occurring and it may be irreversible. What he said was stupid as an observation, but as a prophecy it may have been an act of genius."

"Aren't observations always flawed?" I asked.

"Of course, of course, but we are nothing else. If we floated in an environment that sustained us but cut us off from our senses, our brains would be useless. Everything we are is the product of experience, but as our observations are always partial and often false, we all exist in a state of delusion. That's another point. That's the real purpose of our existences – to battle with that deficiency. But we probably shouldn't battle with it, should we? We should accept it,

73

but probe all the same."

"So freedom to some extent is about ourselves?"

"To a very great extent," he smiled.

"And society is there to test us; we should accept it as a puzzle we have to solve. Or at the very least, freedom concerns the individual not the society."

"Not entirely. Society cannot create freedom, but it can create an environment in which freedom can prosper. A good society should not attempt to mould its citizens in the manner of *homo sovieticus* or *homo oeconomicus*, which is the Western equivalent. A good society should allow its citizens to develop their own multiple, contrasting and interdependent personalities, which assist the commonweal through an unending and unendable debate.

"A good society should not encourage its citizens to want things, but at the same time it should not have them wanting of things. For there is no freedom for those who are in want of the essentials of life, and there is no freedom for those who are prey to insatiable and unnecessary wants."

He smiled again and then gently descended into sleep, depriving me of the chance to take my leave, but that would have been very difficult. He had said so much and yet I wasn't immediately aware of how this encounter would affect me in the months and years to come. A few days later, the good professor told me in his matter-of-fact manner that the dying man was now dead, having survived so little time from our meeting and long before his hoped-for target of the 19th of September. When the result did come in, I thought of him and was glad that he did not make it – all that struggle to survive only to hear what for him would have been bad news.

VII

What the Presbyterian Minister and
the Russian Mystic Had to Say

Maryanne abandoned her appointments to speak on panels and I abandoned the good professor and his itinerary of enlightened minds. We extended our sojourn in the Highlands, which we drove around in a hire car courtesy of the newspaper. I justified this by sending out regular articles, which she spiced up with a few anecdotes of her own or ones she'd heard. They became part of our routine. At night we slept in each other's arms, entangled in manners that should have caused discomfort but never did. In the morning we rose early but unbidden, as though to a plan we dreamt during our slumbers, and went out for walks with an aimless purposefulness, though I now know that the demons that drove each of us were very different.

She spoke of politics as if it could change the nature even of the heather we trudged, whilst I barely listened and heeded only the honeyed air[17] in my lungs, the weak sun, the damp, and of course her presence. To my foreign eyes, the strange light appeared to reveal a new understanding distant and more eternal than the endless talk of votes, tactics, lies and ideals that dominated the discourse of those days. She was part of something that would or could be,

---

[17] Cinico appears to be untypically transported at this point. I translated his *aria melata* as "honeyed air" which works well, I think, but he may have chosen the English "mellifluous". He would have rejected *mellifluo* which has the suggestion of false or inauthentic sweetness.

and I felt freed from something in the past that had trapped me from I couldn't remember when – from birth perhaps.

We climbed across the endless emptiness of a green and often sodden desert, gaining summits that revealed lochs that beckoned and scattered pools, endless iterations that dazzled because they defied the logic of land and its exploitation. At home, I would have had to climb above two thousand metres to see such desolation, and still this was different. Our mountains are hostile, yet tamer in their rugged extremes. Maryanne seemed unimpressed by what she saw. Perhaps that's what a nation is: a place that its natives cannot see.

We enjoyed each other's company, even though we walked in different lands: I in a wonderland that belonged to us and she in a landscape defined by history. She talked of clearances, battles and abandoned villages, as though I could understand the human geography of a land bereft of signs of human habitation beyond the occasional broken wall. My imagination failed me, and in my elation it didn't seem to matter. We made love in the woods or with unnecessary modesty beside a wall of rock. We sought each other out with a hunger that now seems absurd but then felt like a force of nature, whose source could never be exhausted. It felt like the start of something new rather than the ephemeral blast of something never understood and now ungraspable, distant and perhaps never entirely real.

No folly can last forever, but in a better world it could – or could at least last for a goodly while.

I gave in to the good professor's attempts to contact me on my mobile phone. I could see that Maryanne was becoming restless. The campaign was carrying on without her, and while I could quite happily have continued to sample the B&Bs and guest houses of north-west Scotland for months on end in her company, I was not willing to put the relationship at risk. We weren't quite ready to allow time away from each other, so as a transition I agreed to accompany her to the Isle of Lewis where she was talking on a panel with Jim Paterson. Of course, the good professor was furious with me and claimed that the newspaper had also been upset by my negligence, which of course was a lie, but I didn't challenge him. The important thing was to get him to agree to our itinerary, which proved to be quite simple: "Yes, it's important that you see the Hebrides. They're an integral part of our Scottish heritage." I immediately thought that his words must have been the politically correct thing to say: the token by which such people always remember to tick the box but would be up in arms if central government started to spend real money on improving the infrastructure of such places. Not that I knew anything about the islands, but islands are by their nature remote and often neglected. It turned out that the European Union had done more for their roads in twenty years than the British state had done in two hundred. So much for the nation state as a true community.

George appeared to attach great importance to his role, which was strange: his friend David Finlayson had given him an accurate assessment of Il Messaggio del Popolo's standing in the Italian newspaper firmament, and the editor had already established that he was being paid a pittance. According to his own philosophy, we are all governed by our economic self-interest, so he was recklessly ignoring his own credo. I believe that his motivation – quixotic in the extreme – was to persuade his peers that he is someone who gets things done, someone who people have heard of beyond the borders of Scotland and the United Kingdom, rather than what he was: the first Scottish professor of politics our researcher could find, who could be bothered and wasn't too busy. How many of us spend our lives driven by this all too human desire to be accepted and even admired by our own circle? And why do we not realise the futility of it, as every other member of the circle is pursuing that same elusive chimera? However irritating he may have been and however shallow some of his political perceptions, he was undoubtedly useful to me at the time – evidence of something important to the human condition: all types – excepting the violent and the overbearing – are necessary and interact with each other. A humanity constituted entirely of saints would be a dull and possibly even dangerous place. I must be careful here; I'm almost arguing for the best of all possible worlds, which George would no doubt approve of.

I went alone to meet George at Inverness railway station and took him to the ferry in Ullapool. When we boarded, we obviously found Maryanne and I introduced her to George, assuming that he had no recollection, though I knew that she remembered him. The subterfuge was probably unnecessary but lovers are partial to such things and she occasionally kicked me under to table to communicate something – possibly how much she was enjoying the whole encounter. We had sat down together but he seemed unwilling to acknowledge her and expatiated for half an hour on his busy schedule since we last saw each other. In a way, he explained, it had been serendipitous that I had disappeared off the face of the earth, because in any case he'd been recalled to Edinburgh on urgent business. Maryanne bided her time.

"Professor," she said eventually, "I have the feeling that you're going to vote No. I'm undecided, so perhaps you're the one to explain the arguments in favour of No." I had noticed that she was no longer wearing her Yes badge, and could sense the provocation coming.

"Gladly, young lady," he replied, "the first and most important reason is economic. Scotland simply wouldn't be viable as an independent state. This nonsense about petroleum is quite irresponsible. After all Scotland exports more to England than it does to the European Union."

"And it wouldn't be able to export to England after independence?"

"Well, you can't expect the English to be nice to you, if you up sticks and leave them." George liked the odd cricketing metaphor, though I doubt he ever played the game.

"And would Europe be nice to Britain if it left the EU?"

"Ah! There we're in agreement, young lady, this madness in the Conservative Party about Europe."

"Professor Lovenight, it's very kind of you to keep calling me young lady, but I'm not a lady and not that young. I'm thirty-three."

"That's young from where I sit," he chortled proudly from his years, and I swear that I heard him suppress another "young lady".

"I suppose," she said, continuing to reel him in, "that's why we shouldn't expect the English to allow us to use their pound."

"That's correct," he puffed and paused, and looked slightly lost, uncertain whether she was agreeing or disagreeing with him.

"Interesting. It's all much clearer now, but there is one thing that attracts me to a Yes vote," she paused to look at his expression, which only betrayed a trace of suspicion. "You see, the SNP believes in immigration and so do I, but the Westminster parties are all against it to some degree. They keep saying that we're an overcrowded island, but we're not and we need immigrants. Besides there is a moral and legal imperative to welcome asylum seekers."

He smiled as though he felt that his arguments in this department were particularly well practised: "I'm all for tolerance and we are a tolerant nation, but the problem with Britain is that it has become too tolerant. It is now guilty of what we can only call passive tolerance. For too long we have been saying to our citizens and more especially to those who come to live amongst us that we'll leave them alone as long as they obey the law. By doing this we have abdicated our right to protect our own quite unique values. We must now enact active tolerance."

He smiled again, this time triumphantly, and she, who for some reason had been holding back, decided that this was the one. This one was different. This one was going to be fun. "What exactly do you mean by tolerance?" she asked.

He was irritated and, suppressing another "young lady", he said, "I think we all know what tolerance means. To allow, I would say. To put up with, we might say in everyday language."

"Exactly, it's the second one. It comes from the Latin, 'to endure'. You put up with something because you have no right to intervene. You may have the means of coercion, the police, the army, or whatever, but you make a moral decision not to use them because there is no reason to. It is not enough that you disagree with what someone is saying or doing, in part because you cannot be sure that you're right and they're wrong. This is called tolerance, and started with tolerance of other religions and then political ideas. It should be the cornerstone of liberal society."

"Young lady, don't lecture me. I was at university when you were ..."

"For Christ's sake, get a grip! What do you mean 'active tolerance'? Nothing. You haven't even thought those words out. It's like saying, 'cold snow'. Snow is cold; it doesn't need the adjective. Have you ever heard of hot snow? Tolerance is passive. It allows, as you said, but more meaningfully it allows what the tolerant persons find unpleasant or disagreeable in some manner depending on their degree of tolerance. We don't have to tolerate what we like, we embrace it effortlessly. Absolute tolerance would allow everything. If active tolerance could exist, then that's what it would be, but you don't mean that. Absolute tolerance is only possible for a few highly religious or perhaps philosophical people who will never be around for long."

"So you would allow people to disobey the law."

She looked exasperated. It's only amusing to win an argument when your opponent can understand his error. "Of course not. I don't believe in absolute tolerance; I believe in the tolerance of everything that is allowed by the law, but I retain my own right to argue against what I think is wrong. And others should be tolerant of that. Tolerance is precisely what you said passive tolerance is: we leave people alone as long as they obey the law. And I'm all for it. This is not some inferior kind of tolerance, it is quite simply the only thing tolerance is. You New Labour people want to be one thing and the other. You want to call yourselves tolerant and act intolerantly to those who don't agree with you. Worst of all, you pander to the xenophobic rumblings from the right. You use your weird definitions to justify unjust policies which others argue for more honestly."

"We don't use the term New Labour any more."

"You may not, but I do. You slapped the label on the Labour Party, and now you tell us not to use it. It's a good label, because it's says exactly what's in the bottle: something that is no longer what it was."

I stood up at this stage and walked off to get a drink at the bar, thus infuriating them both. She sat down on the stool quarter of an hour later, and took another couple of minutes before she could speak, which I used to get her the drink she clearly needed. "What happened to you?" she asked.

"I went off to tolerate some other people. It was getting difficult to endure you two, but I liked the Latin etymology. You certainly put him on the spot."

"But he's so fucking stupid. You can't get through to people like that."

"You've been in this world for thirty-three years; you must have met a few like that."

"Not like that. He's intolerable."

"I thought that you were all for tolerance. Exercise it."

"And you're a sanctimonious bastard," and she lifted her glass with a grin.

It was a bright spring afternoon when we arrived in Stornoway.

The town is a natural port you arrive at along a fjord or "sea loch" as they call them here. The terrain is low-lying and in parts boggy with rocky outcrops, and there's a scattering of townships – more populated than many parts of the Highlands and Islands. When it docks, the ferry feels like a floating bell as its clanging sounds echo in the ship's metal shell. The ships carry some of the area's desolation within them, but more than anywhere else in the region, Stornoway asks that important question, "What would it be like to live here?"

Partly it's the population, as there's more people living at the top of an Italian alp than in the wide valleys of the Highlands, some of which look quite fertile. And partly it's the paradox that precisely this extended bogland is where the largest community has survived. To the south in Harris or to the west in Uig, you can see that the hills and the stretches of stunningly white sands could seduce people to live there, but in fact few do. There are levels of isolation no Italian could understand.

The town, which accounts for about half the population of the island, is not exactly bustling, but it feels like a real place and not a theatre set created for tourist consumption, though a little desultory tourism does pass by. These are perhaps the more discerning tourists who wish to tour where others don't go. There is the occasional foreign number plate, which infers that some are willing to go to great lengths to enjoy the unpredictable pleasures of this wet and windy isle.

And the town, though not free of a certain drabness, has an engaging archaism about its businesses and the services they provide. It can boast a surprisingly good restaurant and a characterfully neglected pub, but next to Stornoway, my own modest native town of Lugo does start to shine. Yet context has to be taken into account. You don't come to the very edge of Northern Europe in search of consumer heaven. Even a hard-boiled, city-living cynic like myself has to admit that there's something fascinating, even noble about these small societies surviving and sometimes even flourishing where, it seems to me, human beings were never intended to live. This is not just Northern Europe, which could start around a hundred kilometres south of Paris, and it's not just northern Northern Europe, which could be Glasgow – a place that I consider to have a pretty hostile climate; it is the northern rim of Northern Europe, where curious cultures cling to life struggling against the centralising forces of global capitalism and consumer society.

In this part of the world, they speak Gaelic – just as they speak Slovenian or Albanian in some parts of Italy, though many Italians don't know that. It's like Irish, but they insist that it's a different language and apparently it was spoken over almost all of Scotland once and even into north-western England. I heard some of their songs, and I can confirm that it has nothing to do with English.

I left Maryanne on the ferry to find her own way to her lodgings and meet up the organisers of her event, and I drove George to his hotel, where I parked and went off alone to soak up the atmosphere of the place. It wasn't going to take long, as the centre of the Hebridean capital consists of a tiny grid of three or four streets running each way. You could familiarise yourself with it in half an hour, yet everything is there including an arts centre and, like Rome, a church every few yards, with the difference that here each one belongs to a different denomination. This was the clearest sign of the island's famed religiosity. To some extent I was tired of the referendum, and the idea of returning to the hotel to meet yet another group of New Labour politicians and worthies did not attract me. George had given me a few addresses, and one was of a priest[18]

---

[18] "priest": De Oblivii continues to call the minister a priest, as most Italians do when referring to Protestant ministers, as they fail to see the distinction [editor's note].

or "minister" as they call them in the Scottish churches. They live in what is termed a manse, and the one I arrived at was an imposing building by the standards of the island. Inside there was a large hall and a grand staircase, which demonstrated that these men must once have been powerful figures. The floors were of course carpeted from wall to wall, as is the custom in Britain, but the carpets looked as though they hadn't been changed in a long time; they were faded but not worn, and perhaps this unmarried priest had had few visitors. I was taken into the sitting room, which was a large, sturdy room whose studied grandeur had been drained of all vigour and colour. Two large armchairs and a sofa failed to fill the space, and there was a writing desk against one of the walls. The priest stood up and revealed himself to be a tall, gangly man with a sombre demeanour. He was polite in a minimalist fashion, and looked as though he fed on no more than a dried piece of toast and a glass of water a day. His gaunt face gave prominence to a large aquiline nose, which in English is often referred to as a Roman nose. I suppose that it's more common in Mediterranean countries. There was no smile and no surprise that an Italian journalist had wandered into his home. He didn't shake my hand but simply gestured to the other armchair.

A large fireplace was burning coal and the heat roasted one side of my body, while the other experienced an arctic blast that had somehow conquered the manse's ancient defences. We sat in silence awhile, and he studied my card which his housekeeper had given him.

"Mr De Oblivii," he said eventually as though he wanted to test out the sound of my name, "you are travelling in Scotland to cover the referendum?" He sculpted the words as we do in our language, but unlike the British and more particularly the English who run them together.

"Yes," I replied in a surprisingly small voice that took me unawares. The man had spooked me without my realising it.

"You are interested in the referendum, but you have come to a man of God?"

Every statement sounded like a question or perhaps an expression of incredulity. I attempted to laugh and shifted in my armchair, "I understand what you mean, but I am also telling my readers about Scotland, which they know little about."

"They haven't heard of Scotland?"

"No, ... I mean, they have heard of it. I'm sure that many have heard of it, but quite a few don't know that much about it," I squirmed.

"I visited Florence and Rome once."

"And did you enjoy your stay?" I asked looking for a break in the clouds.

"The Italians eat too much, I think," was all of his reply.

"The art?"

"Very skilled, you can be sure of that, but not appropriate for the house of God. The Bible is very clear."

Italy was not proving to be a very unifying subject, and Italians take for granted that people will say good things about them, particularly if they mention art. I was impressed by – perhaps even appreciative of – the priest's refusal to bow before the altar of Leonardo and Michelangelo. It seemed original, though it may have been ancient prejudice.

"I came because I wanted to know more about religion on the islands. Is it as strong as it used to be?"

"It is as strong as God ordains it to be. I never question His will."

"I have heard that ferries couldn't run on a Sunday. Did you agree with that?"

"Of course. And I still demand that they bring an end to this violation of the Sabbath."

"But if a referendum endorsed the decision to have them on a Sunday, you would then accept that decision?"

"I'm not interested in democracy. Politics is part of this world which is only a preparation for the next. I'm interested in the word of God – I'm interested in the Bible." I realised in that moment that I was in the presence of something stunningly archaic: a voice from another century. This was not religion in the happy-clappy, Jesus-loves-you, let's-get-our-guitars-out-and-have-a-sing-song way; this was religion as it must have been. Religion with hard edges, founded on the fear of God. I wished that I could speak with him, even learn from him. Not to adopt his Bible-thumping certainties, but at least to understand them from a great distance. But that distance was too great. We did not have a common language of ideas with which to bridge it. The Highlands and Islands are hospitable places, and no sooner are you in someone's house, which happens more often there than anywhere else in Scotland, than that someone has shoved a cup of weak, milky tea and a piece of cake in your hand, but here there was no sign of it. I had been expecting the house-keeper to come in at any moment with an unasked-for tray heavy with boiling liquids and food with high sugar content. But it failed to arrive, and I realised that our conversation, unsatisfactory as it was, had nowhere else to go.

I stood up to take my leave and held out my hand. He appeared not to see it, but said in a voice that expressed sadness that I think was not intended, "Thank you for coming, my Italian friend. Whatever your religion, remember to read your Bible, and if you do that, you will not go far wrong." Having done his pastoral duty, he turned to look at the fire, and whether he was a soul at peace or a soul in torment I could not tell you.

I come from a quite anticlerical town in an anticlerical region. We were once part of the Papal States, and we were not fond of a Catholic Church that was often our landowner and always our temporal power and our tax collector, but now I see that Catholicism is a religion *all'acqua di rosa*.[19] It's

---

[19] *all'acqua di rosa*: literally "like rose water" but in the sense that it is very watered down.

like whisky that you buy in the shop, while this man's religion is one hundred per cent on volume. It doesn't get any stronger. I think that even in his own church, he must be a bit of a loner, a figure they perhaps respect but shun, as no one today can or should live with unending gloom, though our age perhaps tends towards unending frivolity and I've had a pretty good go at it myself. I left the manse, and on the pavement outside two middle-aged drunks passed, effing and blinding as they went, proving what I had already guessed: the man inside was a Calvinist Mohican. His was the hoarse voice of a conflict that had enflamed Europe four or five centuries ago. Leaving aside the academic question of who was in the right – if anyone was – there has to be something heroic in that. Perhaps the most heroic people are those who first enunciate an idea and those who, centuries later, are the last ones to defend it.

I rose quite early in the morning so that I could see a bit more of the town and still be in time for breakfast at the good professor's hotel. He was drinking his coffee and seemed in affable mood.

He did say, "Who was that dreadful woman you introduced me to on the ferry?" but when I replied vaguely, "She's campaigning for the Yes side and sometimes speaks at events. Women for Independence, I think," he showed absolutely no interest. She and her kind could not be taken seriously, and were beyond discussion. This was another noticeable difference between the two campaigns: Yes had a powerful urge to proselytise, while No was just offended by the very idea of independence. It made little attempt to analyse the political forces driving Yes, at least until the closing weeks of the campaign, and then only in a cursory manner.

I told him of the minister I'd met, though I kept calling him a priest. It's difficult for us to drop that term. George was niggled by the story. He didn't like the idea of a foreigner seeing what was after all an integral part of Scottish history – one that he would like to forget as someone proud of being British and proud of being Scottish. He obviously hadn't heard of the Borgias and the other skeletons in our cupboard. More significantly he didn't understand that I liked the priest. Unlike me he believed in something. His world was understandable to him.

George's face suddenly brightened: "If you're in the mood for visiting religious weirdos, I have just the man for you." And he produced the business card of a Russian mystic who was living in a restored black house in a remote part of Lewis. "How do you find out about these things?" I cried with genuine admiration. The Russian was travelling the world and stopping at selected remote places where he would stay for six months, a year or even two years on occasions. It was hardly relevant to the referendum, but George thought it might have been newsworthy. I was more intrigued than I had been with his other ideas, though they had often proved to be more entertaining than expected. This one could prove to be the other way round. George was too busy to come, as he often was, though I never fathomed what he was busy at. Networking, I suppose.

I drove out to the Russian's black house, a long and low, grim construction in unworked stones with a thatched roof and hardly any windows. Light rain was falling on a dull evening, and I had come to the end of the world. I knocked on the flimsy door, and it was eventually opened by a smartly dressed young woman whose accent declared her to be Russian as soon as she spoke in a precise but awkward English.

"This way for holy man," she said, certain that I shared her awe, instead of being a hack unaccustomed to awe of any kind. This way was not very far: the inside of a black house is smaller than expected because of the thickness of the walls, which consist of two thick drystone walls whose cavity is filled with earth and stones. You entered a tiny hall and on the right there was a large room which had once been used for cattle – what they call a "byre". I never entered that room, and I suspect that that was where the modern stuff was kept: the computers, telephones, printers, televisions and the like. I was led into the room on the left, which was a bedroom and living area, exactly as it would have been in the old days. The bed must have been an original, as it looked like a badly made cupboard, but had an opening two metres high and three metres wide, and a curtain that wasn't drawn, so it revealed a bed of straw with a flimsy sheet on top. There was a small wooden table with a samovar on top – the only clearly Russian item in the room. Everything spoke of holy poverty – the rundown version of a Shaker household. He sat in a roughly made chair of immense proportions, which gave it the look of a rustic throne. He wore a contrite expression which suggested not remorse but discomfort at being torn from his meditations. He nodded to me to sit on a small sofa, the only item of furniture that looked manufactured and post-war. The one thing that didn't speak of poverty was him, a big, well-fed man who looked as though he pumped iron for two hours early in the morning rather than flagellating himself with a knotted rope and crying out to God for forgiveness.

"What can I do for you?" he said in a dull voice, and it sounded like a question he asked often.

"Just a talk," I replied, "just a few questions about your work and why you made this interesting decision to travel the world."

He looked confused and took a long time to reply. "I am here to help lost sheep on the road to faith, and not to bare my soul."

"No, please don't bare your soul. That wasn't my intention. I was just wanting to find out about this …," I wasn't sure what word to use, "… adventure of yours. Your decision seems a very remarkable one – a brave one. You understand."

"Find out? No, I don't understand," he stared at me as

though confronted with something dangerous, possibly evil. "Who are you?"

"My name is Cinico de Oblivii, and I'm a journalist for *Il Messaggio del Popolo*. I'm in Scotland reporting on the referendum," and I held out my card to him.

He took it, and he too studied it for some time: "There's a referendum?"

"Yes, didn't you know that?"

"Why should I know that? Why would I want to know that?"

"Do you get many lost sheep?"

"Enough."

"Enough for what?"

"Enough."

"Do you succeed in saving any of them?" I asked without interest, because the conversation had gone off in a direction that was entirely alien to me and I could no longer think.

"No, of course not."

"How do you mean, of course not? Why are you doing it then?"

"To save my own soul, which I hold very dear. I must show willing to the Lord my master."

"But why can't they be saved?"

"Because their souls have been corrupted. Not only that, they have lost their souls."

"Lost their souls? What does that mean?"

"It is like coffee," he paused, as though expecting me to ask why. I refused and held his stare. Eventually he looked away and adopted an even more meditative pose. "Black coffee can always be turned into white coffee, simply by adding milk – to taste, of course."

"And?"

"But white coffee clearly cannot be turned back into black coffee. The process is irreversible."

"Meaning?"

Again a pause – this time of surprise.

"I would have thought that intelligent man like you would have grasped that thought as it flew through the air," he looked uncomfortable with my continuing presence, as though I were no longer worthy of his company, "with dexterity of tennis player, like one you're so proud of – what's his name? Andy Murray?"

"I'm Italian, not Scottish."

"So you are! I forgot and it's not easy to tell Western Europeans apart."

"Really? Aren't we divided north and south – by latitude and not longitude?"

"That's such a Western European thing to say. Of course Europe is divided east and west. Western European no longer has soul; Western European is no more than consumption machine. Small machine for making money circulate. Small machines will never regain souls they've lost. It is like coffee, as I've already told you. Now you're white coffee, and you'll never again have good strong taste of coffee as it should be drunk. You're insipid. As Eastern Europeans are now being seduced by consumer society, they too will lose their souls, but this hasn't happened yet. At least, it has only just started to happen, and we must struggle to stop it from happening."

"Ah, I see what you mean. Not entirely, but I get the coffee bit."

"So you're happy now, you can leave me in peace. I have my work to do."

"I understand, but what is that work? If the lost sheep can't be unlost."

He conceded himself a small chuckle, which revealed a glimpse of someone entirely different hidden behind the theatre. "You think that you're funny, because like all Western Europeans, you can only be flippant. There is no gravitas. Nothing that could be considered important enough to bind us together: religion, politics, humanity. Everything is game for you, even war is game. War is monstrous, but war as game is even worse, because no one sees it for what it really is."

"We have been talking for some time, but I feel that I know less about you than I did when I came into the room."

"That is point," he smiled, "what is understood or, worse, familiar is contemptible."

I felt at this stage that he was the one with games, and I couldn't understand what they were. I decided to take the interview in a more conventional direction. "What's your background in Russia? You look to me to be around forty …"

"Forty-seven," he interrupted not without a hint of vanity.

"Well then, you were brought up in the Soviet Union. What did your father do?"

"He was high-up communist official. Nomenklatura, you would say."

"We would say?"

"Yes, you in the West always talk about nomenklatura, but this is everywhere. In West you call your nomenklatura 'networking'. Same thing – identical; it's nomenklatura with glass of wine in its hand."

"And the nomenklatura didn't partake of the odd vodka when they met?"

"Oh they did, they did, but word itself is not suggestive of that, while 'networking' is."

"Do you regret the passing of the Soviet Union?"

"No, but I had good life in Russia then. And I have not bad life now. I think it was better then, but its passing, you say, made me think about what was wrong. My father was good communist and now he is good capitalist. He owns factory and is multimillionaire with house in Rome. Now that I seek God, government and system are not important to me. I think that you must be going."

"Very well," I said, "it has been interesting." And I stood up to go.

He did not stand up, but addressed me forcefully, "Mr Cinico, I normally charge thirty pounds for quarter of hour in my presence, you are slightly over that time, but we can agree to thirty pounds."

"Thirty pounds? I couldn't do that. The paper would never reimburse me, and what have I got out of this?"

"You got whatever you want to make of it."

"I couldn't pay you, as it would be bad for your soul."

He chortled again, but said, "I live in capitalist system, and I need to eat. I have my team as well to think of."

"Your team? It's a strange anchorite who has a team. No doubt you have a Facebook page."

"Of course, how else would I find my customers? I am not rich, Mr Cinico, as I do not speak to my father. This is all I have."

He didn't seem put out that I wasn't paying him. He remains the most enigmatic person I have ever met, but that perhaps was what he was dealing in: enigmas. Some may say that this proves that our economic system provides whatever there is demand for, but what I find more remarkable is the manner in which people adapt when there is no choice.

On my return to the hotel, I found the good professor at the bar. I told him the story of the Russian, and he answered succinctly, "Nutjob, then?" I have noted in Britain that people make little use of register, but they all, including university professors, suddenly come out with the condensed jargon of youth with no sense of incongruity. It contrasted weirdly with the Russian whose lifestyle was a cross between medieval piety and Harvard Business School.

"Maybe," I replied, "but he has a point. I think that perhaps in the West we have lost our souls, and that the post-Cold-War, east-west divide is now deeper than the historic divide between Northern and Southern Europe."

VIII

What the Italian Professor and my Father Had to Say

One evening while Maryanne busied with her next talk, and I lazed waiting for the deadline to come closer before I got to grips with an article on the 22nd of May European election and yet another on the Scottish referendum, whose new angle was difficult to find, I received a phone call from my aunt telling me that my father was dying. She was very blunt, and I was more sensitive to the subtext which cried out loud against the miserable son I was to my father and the uncaring father I was to my daughter. And certainly the latter was true. I was not even then without a sense of guilt. Who is? But that guilt never altered my behaviour.

This time there was no escape; I had to return to Italy. Maryanne was disconcertingly eager to release me, and said, "my love" as she convinced me of the importance of familial relations. Don't worry, she reassured me, we would soon get back to normal, once I was back, though I was not convinced. We were still on the island after five days. Even George had left, and we were in limbo. It was time to get on with the practicalities of life, but we were unable to make decisions. The phone call was opportune for her, and I had been conscious of her increasing restlessness.

At the Heathrow departure lounge on my way to Italy, I saw a man strutting around the airport in a pair of baggy trousers, bright yellow trainers and a T-shirt that broadcasted a message in English from his chest to an increasingly anglophone world – an assertion of bold *menefreghismo*: "They're going to judge me anyway, so whatever." Whether he understood the content of his shirt or not, his behaviour suggested that he probably did follow the dictates of its rudimentary philosophy.

Something about him suggested that he was a countryman of mine – possibly the fact that every now and then he grabbed his own genitalia and gave them a good scratch, even to the extent of thrusting his hand under the loose material of his strange trousers better to make sure that he did a proper job of it. Then he raised his iPhone and entered a number quickly, "Eh! Finocchio, che fin hai fatto?"[20] he shouted for the benefit of any Italian speakers who happened to be around. This confirmed his national origins and suggested that the Italy I was flying back to after twelve years away would be different from the one I had left. No one, not even this kind of Italian I always avoided, would have dressed in yellow shoes and Indian-print pyjamas. "Campa cavallo,"[21] he shouted as though to remind me that some things wouldn't have changed.

I was returning to our country after an inexcusably long absence. This was, I admit, a terrible lapse for a son, a father and an Italian. I didn't plan it that way, but I could never see any pressing reason for returning and simply postponed my familial duties until it became difficult to imagine how this could happen. A spell was formed and it was difficult to break.

The greatest cultural shock comes when a person returns to their own country after a long time, precisely

---

[20] *Eh! Finocchio, che fin hai fatto?*: "Hey, you pansy, where have you been hiding?"

[21] *Campa cavallo*: the literal meaning of the Italian expression "Campa cavallo, l'erba cresce," is "The horse lives on and the grass grows," but its actual meaning is "Time moves on and nothing much changes." The expression is so current in Italian culture that the first two words are now sufficient.

because they're not expecting it: the language has changed, the fashions and obsessions have changed, familiar buildings have disappeared and many news ones have been put up, the political parties have changed (particularly in Italy) but not all the politicians (particularly in Italy), and above all the whole way of thinking has changed. It's as though the country has quietly decided to become a completely different country behind your back. Of course much has remained the same, but instead of reassuring, it appears to give greater prominence to those changes. Those who return home every six months or even every year can adjust to the changes gradually, and in a sense they never leave, even if those visits are brief. After twelve years, it's a shock. You get over it quickly, but the initial impact is unforgettable.

My aunt had said that my father wanted to talk to me one last time. The invite was not one I could refuse, but nor was it one that augured well. Why rush towards the torture chamber? By the time I was on the shuttle train from Fiumicino Airport to the centre of Rome, I discovered almost through some unconscious revelation that I could at least postpone it. I imagined him in bed dying like the man I had recently met, but instead of lying still, looking at the ceiling and reflecting on life, my father could not stop gesticulating and staring accusations at me, whilst he spoke incessantly and I listened to not a word of it. Somehow this dish did not look particularly palatable, and I decided to make a detour.

My patron and friend was no longer the professor of politics at Rome University; he had got himself one of those plum jobs we all dream of: the directorship of the Viterbo Campus of the University of Southern Illinois. I hadn't been in touch for a number of years, even by e-mail, but had heard of this cushy number. I was not surprised. In Glasgow someone told me the expression, "If he fell in the Clyde, he'd come up with a salmon in his mouth."[22] And I thought immediately of my patron. An expression of unalloyed disdain for almost everything can take you a long way in life.

In the age of smartphones, no one is more than a few minutes away from someone else, if that no one has the someone's name and place, as well as the sudden desire to make contact. I spoke to the telephonist and I spoke to my one-time protector, who greeted me with guarded friendliness. Of course I should come. *Che bella sorpresa!*[23] He used the word "spontaneous" as though it were a virtue, but not without the suggestion that for the Director of the Viterbo Campus it should be kept within limits.

When I got to Viterbo railway station, I discovered that the campus was in fact quite distant from Viterbo, around fifty kilometres of Lazio's countryside and up into the hills. The expensive taxi ride gave me a little time to reflect on my rashness, but when I saw the campus buildings, I was won over. I have no idea what the architecture of the real Southern Illinois campus is like or indeed where it could be on the map and which post-industrial city it may belong to, but the Viterbo subsidiary is gorgeous. I come from the flatlands of Romagna, and here was postcard Italy: not just the hills, the vineyards and the olive groves, but also a *palazzo signorile*[24] with a renaissance garden. The main building was stunning, if a little over-restored for university purposes. Glass screens and walkways conflicted with the whole, but it was probably on the verge of ruin when the university bought it. Europe is changing once more, and there appear

---

[22] The author appears to have mistranslated this Glaswegian expression, though he may just have wanted to adapt it to Italian. The version in his text, *Se cascasse nel fiume, acchiapperebbe un salmone tra i denti*, means "If he fell in the river, he would catch a salmon with his teeth."

[23] *gesto spontaneo* in the original.

[24] *palazzo signorile*: a country house in this case.

like mushrooms new forces, new hierarchies, new cultures and new economies, some of which are hidden from view, and this was part of that wider change, I felt sure.

I was dropped at the gate by the taxi, and was encumbered with luggage for a week-long trip. The gate was offensively large, its pillars recently plastered and painted, and there was a buzzer, which I pressed.

"Chi è?" someone asked aggressively in an American accent.

I answered in English that I had an appointment with the director, and the voice immediately changed in tone. I was advised which door I should approach for the reception and then the gate clicked open. As the wheels of my suitcase struggled against the gravel and I took in the size of the building and the curve of the steps leading to both sides of the facade, further regrets began to surface and even a little guilt. Even a cynic like myself can feel that a wrong decision turns out to be wrong because it was at its inception immoral, but this thought, at least in my case, only occurs when reality illumines its underlying stupidity, which is the most likely reason for things going wrong or a sense that they may do very soon. In other words, I would rather admit that there's a moral dimension to the universe than concede that I may occasionally act like a fool. And even I could not be immune to the startling paradox that only recently had I visited the deathbed of a man I had never known in health, while I was now doing all I could to avoid the deathbed of my own father. The thought that I had a slightly unpleasant nature lingered.

The efficient, non-geographic woman at reception effortlessly produced a have-a-nice-day smile and said with equal predictability, "Good afternoon. Mr De Oblivii, isn't it?" The "isn't it" denoted, I thought, the unofficial nature of my visit. It implied that she didn't have to know because I hadn't gone through the right channels. "The professor will be down in a minute."

Twenty-five minutes later the professor breezed in. He allowed himself a grin, and opened his arms to suggest an embrace that was not intended. "Chi non muore, si rivede," he said.[25] I smiled back a friendly but confident smile. After all, I was no longer a supplicant. "Pino, ti vedo ben pasciuto e pronto per un'illustre vecchiaia."[26] And I even entertained the idea of patting him on the back. His smile was checked, and we looked at each other like two strangers. Too many years had passed by and old selves had been left far behind.

"Cinico," he said as we climbed the stairs to his palatial office in an attempt to recapture some of the informality we'd failed to create, "always a sly dog, you've even managed to get here in time for lunch. We'll have an aperitif in my study and then go for some food. The postgraduates come along as well; I'd like you to meet them."

A waiter came with two aperitifs on a tray. And once he had a drink in his hand, the professor – or should I say Pino, now my peer – seemed to relax. "You're following the Scottish referendum, I hear."

"It's interesting, perhaps the most interesting or at least unexpected thing I've covered."

"Really? It's just England you know."

"That's what I thought, but now I'm …"

"I never thought that you would be the one to fall for that nationalist nonsense. It's very nineteenth century."

I sensed that it was best to let the matter drop, and I was myself conflicted over the significance of the referendum. From a distance it now seemed more significant, but my thoughts were still evolving. We were just managing to get

[25] *Chi non muore, si rivede*: "Those who haven't died always show up again" is another common Italian expression.

[26] *Pino, ti vedo ben pasciuto e pronto per un'illustre vecchiaia*: "Pino, you're looking well fed and ready for an illustrious old age." "ben pasciuto" can also be a euphemism for "fat".

on, so I switched the conversation to him: "You've clearly landed on your feet."

"*Certo*," he smiled, "I always have. We even have a budget for art acquisitions."

"But it's not Ivy League," I said with the lack of tact I must have acquired on my travels. Or perhaps it's that journalists, whatever their faults, are straight-talking people. We have no airs and graces; we speak to all kinds of people and we have to learn how to speak to them as equals.

"Maybe not, but I wouldn't have it any other way. No one has heard of these people, but they have money. That's the main thing."

Such are the values of our modern university corporations.

Lunch was in another grand room hung with pictures from centuries past, as though the best research could only be acquired in amenable surroundings amongst symbols of a cultured past. I sense that people never see these things if they live with them every day. Art has to surprise, to unsettle, but nothing can surprise or unsettle if it is always there. It becomes part of our affections, and reassures us. It tells us who we are or would want to be.

English was the language of this elite setting, and a stiff affability prevailed. It was like being hugged by a robot, uncomfortable and occasionally painful. A verbatim of the conversation would have appeared to be friendly and even vivacious at times, but the body language and the delivery changed it into something soulless and overcautious. We were introduced with sparkling CVs, but the professor's tone of voice was dull and unconvincing. We remarked on the unremarkable, and took too much time to sit down. The waiter – the only person with any vitality – busied in and out and brought the wine. It was, I have to say, one of the finest I've ever drunk, and apparently came from their own vineyard.

As I let my mind wander and struggled with my own sense of guilt about my father, the conversation came round to the Scottish referendum again. Pino must have said that I was covering it for *Il Messaggio del Popolo*. I heard a strong female voice with a German accent: "Mr De Oblivii, I said, 'What is your paper's view of the referendum?'"

These words struck home and interrupted my reverie or "dwam", as they call it in Scotland. And the question felt appallingly difficult to answer. I was trapped. It occurred to me, perhaps for the first time, that we hadn't even asked ourselves that question. We didn't have a view, did we? My editor had never discussed the matter, and I doubt he knew anything about it. Yet I had been travelling around Scotland off and on for months. Our default was, I suppose, to stick with the status quo, but I was in close relationship with someone strongly committed to the other side. Gradually I had been storing away experiences and formulating, almost unconsciously, my own reflections on what was happening.

"I don't know that we have one. I just report the facts," I replied a little pompously and bought myself a little time.

"Very commendable," said the German, whom I'd now identified. She was the most genial of the company, and seemed keen to make her mark. "But isn't it difficult to remain detached in the midst of such a momentous event?"

"Momentous is overstating it a bit," said Pino.

"I suppose it is," I answered her.

"So who do you think will win?"

"At the moment, it looks like the No campaign has a majority, but come September, I think that the Yes one may have it."

"Never," said Pino, inexplicably upset by this scenario.

"Why would this be?" asked the German.

"It's simply that the No campaign is so lacklustre and relies entirely on its control of the traditional media. The Yes campaign has public meetings constantly running all over the country. It's impossible to say how much effect it's having and whether it will be enough, but when you've seen it up close, it's difficult not to be persuaded that this is a force for change."

"Interesting," said the German, "this is a 1970s campaign up against a 2010s campaign, and you think that the 1970s one could win."

"Exactly," I said.

"I don't think that there's any chance of that happening," sad Pino with great aplomb – the aplomb of someone in the know. Then it seemed ridiculous, but he was right.

I shrugged and for the first time, I felt myself identifying with Scottish independence.

Pino seemed disoriented by my command of English. This was foolish as anyone can learn a language if they go and live in the country, but he had learnt an extensive vocabulary without ever living in an anglophone country for more than a week or two. In a way he was trying too hard. He didn't sound like an Italian. Instead each vowel seemed to have been squeezed and reshaped into something entirely alien to both the English language and the Italian. He wasn't difficult to follow, as he spoke slowly and deliberately while he worked on the squeezing and reshaping. If anything, it was a little distracting, but not unattractive.

The Scottish referendum served to loosen up the conversation a bit, and having had two or three glasses of their excellent wine, guilt about my father and Pino's prickly personality had all but disappeared. I was no longer in academe but talking recklessly as I do when chatting with other journalists. Forgetful of our ways, I was merrier than I should have been just after lunch – and in the confines of hallowed academe, a secular, commercial and sexually liberated monastery. In the context of our conversation on regional accents, I thought it acceptable to remind the professor of his attempt to impersonate my Romagnolo accent, and then I impersonated him impersonating me while failing to conceal his own Roman accent. This linguistic trickery even raised a little laughter and the odd smirk, but the professor did not see the joke. In fact, he looked as though I had offended him. For a second or two, I felt lost as I struggled to identify the means to rectify my lack of judgement. Then I both rebelled against his desire to impose our old relationship and understood something that did not worry me at all: we would never meet again. An attempt to revitalise a friendship had turned into its funeral. He would never forgive my lack of respect – and, let's face it, my ingratitude. Wasn't all my success due to his generosity and patronage?

I had lived so long abroad that I, a Northerner through and through, forgot that Italians do not appreciate their accents being made fun of. Our national language was imposed in relatively recent historical times, and on top of that there's our division into at least three supposedly distinct units. The Northern Italian considers the Central Italian – and in particular the Roman and the Florentine – to be vulgar and invasive, and the Central Italian considers the Northern Italian to be stuffy and conceited. Of course both accusations are true to some extent – to some very small extent, reality always being more nuanced than stereotype. I'm less stuffy than Pino, but then journalists usually are less stuffy than academics. We may be marked by our national or regional characteristics, but we're moulded more comprehensively by professions – and professional similarities transcend mere national boundaries.

The Northerner – or the Padano as the Lega Nord would like to call us – is different from the Central Italian, who in turn differs from the Southern Italian who is not the same as the Sicilian who cannot be confused with the Sardinian. Christ, every town and village would claim to be profoundly different. We're a nation of fragments, but a nation no less. So why, since my travels under the questionable guidance of the good professor, am I increasingly convinced that Scotland really is a distinct nation. It's not that Scotland differs culturally more from England than Lombardy from

Benevento, and it's not that Scotland isn't riven by its own *campanilismo*. It is something indefinable, arcane, elusive. It is something important, so important that I'm not sure what it is.

The Scots are both vulgar and refined, stuffy and expansive. I can say with untypical certainty that it's their vulgarity and expansiveness that attract, and the suggestions of urbanity and stuffiness only add to the attraction: after all, these things should not coexist. Perhaps their alcohol consumption helps this strange alchemy.

"You've changed," Pino said morosely.

"Dear professor, we all change. It would be odd if we didn't."

"No doubt, but you've become a queer fish."

"I've lived abroad. I have adopted foreign ways. How could I not be foreign, now that I'm part foreigner?"

He didn't look happy with my replies. He stiffened, and even looked a little sad – and lost for words.

"*Caro professore*," I came to his assistance, "we shouldn't fall out. Who knows when we'll meet again? I'm quite happy to be considered a queer fish. Indeed I'm glad to have become one, and I owe it all to you. You were the one who made this possible."

I was proud of my magnanimity and expected him to lighten up and be grateful for the lifeline I had thrown him. Again I had failed to understand the isolation of power. He had no desire for reconciliation; quite the opposite, he appeared more troubled. Perhaps he felt that he had been overgenerous and had provided me with the means to act with such self-assurance and free myself from patronage no longer required. Why would a prince embrace a former vassal's insolence? Why should he? Was I a fool to have expected it? I tell myself that I have no memory of what I may have said wrong, but I deceive myself. Above all it was a matter of tone.

Pino disappeared at some stage and then reappeared

with thunder in his eyes. "There's a car leaving for Viterbo in ten minutes. I think that you should take it." And just to make sure he frogmarched me to it and insisted I get in, even though the driver wasn't there yet and it was an oven inside. In spite of myself, I accepted without demur, as though some of his authority still remained. It was his territory after all. I felt no anger, just relief as the university car slid out through the gate, and we headed for Viterbo. I would have to spend the night in Rome.

Nothing in Pino's behaviour surprised me – or even disappointed. He was, as always, predictable and close to the current received wisdom. When I was young, I had thought that he believed in something – that the sincerity he flourished like a flag of freedom was genuine. I had long since understood that this was not the case, as he twisted and turned with every passing fad, using an increasingly tortuous vocabulary to cover up the wholesale discarding of everything he had appeared to hold dear. What right had I to be angry or disappointed? I owed him everything. My career was built on the solid foundation of his lies. He had accumulated considerable political capital and had generously spent some of it in getting me started in journalism. Was I now to judge him from the comfort of a position he had arranged for me? I could reject him and argue with him precisely because society, in as much as it was aware of me, considered me a success.

Our country is studded with these American campuses that are offshoots of their transatlantic parent companies. It would appear that they do no harm and bring in a few jobs – but not many good ones, such as my ex-patron's, as these are mainly dream postings for mid-career American academics. They are also pools of Anglophonia, one of the few growth industries in a crisis-ridden continent. I read that the *Scoti* of Ulster, having conquered parts of the western coast of the country that many centuries later would take their name, colonised the rest of Scotland through conversion, dynastic unions and religious communities, and imposed their Gaelic language. Later still, when the Norman king, William, suppressed the uprisings in the north of England, English refugee aristocrats flooded the Scottish court, changing its culture or at least starting that long process. Could it be that powerful guests are even more dangerous than powerful invaders? The invaders' threat is so obvious, and triggers a powerful reaction. Is this archipelago of English – unimaginable in the previous generation – the start of a process that could destroy our culture? Do I care? I think that I do, but not enough to do anything about it. No one would like to see their culture die, as is occurring with my own Romagnolo dialect, which is actually another neo-Latin language. Languages are predators, and they feed off other languages. When only one is left, it too will die, as there will be no food chain.

When the taxi drove up to my father's modest home, he was standing in the garden waving and his expression was that of a happy child. As I paid the driver, he ran out on to the pavement in a state of irrepressible excitement. "You've come at exactly the right moment," he said with what appeared to be genuine pleasure at seeing me again.

I waited for the taxi to drive off before I said, "I thought you were dying."

"I was, but recovered."

"You could have told me. It has been a long journey."

"I've only just recovered; besides, I felt that you would like to see your old dad again."

"Nobody recovers that fast. You're sprightlier than I am."

"You would be happier if I were dying?"

"No, dad, I wouldn't. Anyway let's go in. What have you been up to?"

"Well, that's what I meant when I said that you've come at the right moment. I have just come up with the most amazing invention."

"Nothing medical or veterinary, I hope."

He ignored the little barb, and possibly didn't understand it, as he may have understood that it really was my hope. He was not good at grasping irony.

"I have decided to think about myself this time. Enough of wanting to help humanity and the economy, this is about money – making money – making myself rich. You've been generous over the years, son, I have always acknowledged that, but nothing compared to how generous I'll be to you, once this little baby has got going." And he tapped his fingers on a plastic bag which contained a large black object.

Nothing had changed – or would change. There are some people who remain utterly loyal to their immutable inner natures throughout their lives without any reference to the outside world – to reality. You have to admire them, even if it is an extreme form of stupidity. I said nothing. I had nothing to say.

"Not convinced yet? Take a look." He removed a computer case from the plastic bag.

"It looks like an oversized computer case," I said.

"It is a computer bag, and it's large because it does more than any other computer bag in the world."

"It only has to do what a computer case has to do."

"I don't think so. Have you heard of Steve Jobs?"

I grunted. The whole world has heard of Steve Jobs, whether they wanted to or not.

"It was design, not invention really. The computer was already there but he wrapped it up in a novel manner that everyone loves. Let me show you mine."

He took all the clutter off the dining room table, and there was a lot of it: books, newspapers, plates, mugs, ashtrays, screwdrivers, antiperspirant, various spectacle cases, an assortment of pens and pencils, notebooks, loose pages and a spoon. I wasn't sure why he was doing this until he flung the case on the empty table. Then with remarkable dexterity he started to unfold the case: it went on forever, and each time doubled its area, eventually taking up most of the space on the table.

He smiled at last and waved his hand over an enormous display of computer, peripherals and paraphernalia. "This covers everything."

The laptop lay at one end, and then in a perfectly worked-out hierarchy of necessity it started with the lead, the mouse, the screen wipes, the dongles, the memory sticks, software CDs, document sleeves, and finally right at the opposite end thin pouches for holding the old-fashioned things: pens, pencils, rubbers and even a pencil sharpener.

"How did you do that?"

"Easy. Just watch," and with the same dexterity he refolded the whole thing back into a computer case. "The clever thing is that once you've opened it, the computer is loose and ready to pick up. What do you think?"

It was clever. There was no doubt about that. But half the stuff was on the way out. He hadn't understood that whatever genius Jobs had – and people argue over it incessantly – it was about simplicity, and this was the opposite of simplicity. You would have to go on a training course to learn to unfold and refold it like my father did. Perhaps if we had taken him more seriously and advised him, he might actually have achieved something.

"It's brilliant, dad. It's weird," and I almost said, "but it has no practical purpose." Instead I said, "and yet it will be popular with some customers."

"More than just some. This is dynamite."

"Possibly."

"Why the scepticism? Besides, I want you to do something for me."

I had forgotten that this would be where it ended. "What's that, dad?"

"I would like you to show this to your friends in London. Everybody goes on about Milan – capital of design and all that stuff. But they're just traditional, behind the curve, stuck in a rut. They understand nothing."

"Are you sure?"

"Of course I am. I went there last week. Do you think that your dad sits around scratching his balls? I have energy, my boy. Even at my age, I get things done. I went there and showed them."

"And what did they say."

His expression changed. "They just laughed."

"Even when they saw how fast you can fold it and unfold it?"

"Particularly when I did that."

"They weren't laughing at you; they were laughing in amazement."

"No, my son, they were laughing at me," he said. "Your father has been around for a very long time. Nothing much gets past your father. ... But in London it'll be different. Everybody goes on about the English: how they're all snobs and think that they still have an empire. How they've fallen behind, and don't think that they're European, but something better, something special. But actually they are. They invented everything, even football. They will understand."

"Dad, you need a businessman, and I don't know any businessmen. Not here and not in London."

"Of course, you do. You're a journalist. An important journalist."

"Dad, I work for *Il Messaggio del Popolo*, not *Corriere della Sera*, which isn't what it used to be either. I mix with the odd politician, but not the ones who could change anything."

He looked completely deflated. The happy child had gone, and was now replaced by an old man. Perhaps he had been seriously ill.

"I see."

"Well, I could try, I suppose, ..."

"No, don't worry. There are more important things to talk about. I'll sort this out on my own. As I always do."

He led me through to his study, as if the invention had

now disappeared from his mind. He sat down behind his desk and started to stuff tobacco into his pipe. He didn't smoke his pipe often, and when he did, it was never a good sign. Once the pipe was alight, he leant back in his chair and relaxed. Without looking me and after exhaling a few good puffs, he said, "It's time to talk about your responsibilities."

"What responsibilities would they be?" I asked disingenuously.

"You know very well. They are two women you have abandoned: your wife and your daughter, now an adolescent. This republic was founded on the values of hard work and the family. I always upheld them and I expected my son to do so, but what you've done is unpardonable. In my day, a man like you was called a scoundrel. And as for your work, you don't appear to do much, yet they shower you with money."

"It's a reasonable salary, but not riches beyond all measure, dad."

"For what you do!"

"What do you want me to do?"

"First, you need to go and see them."

"Do they want that?"

"You abandoned them in 2002, and you're expecting an invite?"

"I am in touch with Elena, you know. She has never once asked me to come round. I was thinking of going to see her."

"Thinking? How generous of you."

"This isn't getting us anywhere."

"You're the one who has to change. I don't have to go anywhere. I've done my bit. I'm an old man."

"So what *do* you want me to do?"

"Life is not a game ..." and at that point my mind drifted off. If ever there was a man who treated life as a game, it was my father, some part of my conscious thought protested. I admire my father's obsessions and otherworldliness. As a reaction against them, I am more practical – or

110

at least I thought I was at the time. An hour in my father's company reminds me of why parenthood is such a bad idea. And our best weapon against our parents' moralising is the off-switch in our ears.

By the time I left the following morning, my father was pacified. Partly because he needed to tap me for a thousand euros ("I'll pay you back in September," he said) and partly because he thought that he had won the argument.

Before leaving, I wanted to take a swing around the main square, where the monument to the First World War ace pilot and native of Lugo, Count Francesco Baracca, soars to the heavens from which he fell. It's impossible to cross that square without encountering people you know even after twelve years away. On my way to a café, I happened upon the son of an old friend of mine, now grown up but just recognisable from his childhood self. I called his name and, after a two-second lapse, he smiled in recognition and hastened towards me: "Cinico! Where did you go? London, I heard. Are you back for long?"

"No, not long, but what are you up to?"

"Every summer I work as a cook in a posh restaurant in Viareggio, and then I travel in the winter."

"You must make a lot of money from the wealthy if you can travel for half a year on it."

"Not really, as I travel in the Third World. You can find strange animals there; they're called human beings."

"Meaning?"

"Human beings, remember them? That's what we were once ... before we became automata."

"Human beings only in the Third World?" I responded sceptically.

"Pretty much. It doesn't matter where you go, Ecuador, Zanzibar, Madras or Samoa, there are people who live because they don't wallow in comfort. Every day they get up and struggle. Everyone needs a bit of struggle in their lives. Not too much, not so much that it crushes them, but enough to make them appreciate what they have, who they know and the nature or cityscape that surrounds them."

"So you've become a philosopher on your travels. I would never have thought it."

He laughed, "I understand. I never was an academic boy."

"I didn't mean …"

"No, no, you're right. No offence taken. Some people learn from books, and some from life. A different intelligence, but I prefer life."

"So do I. I'm just a hack, you know. Not an intellectual. A conjurer with other people's ideas. You've made a good choice."

"I learn from others. We could all learn, if we let more immigrants in. But that'll never happen."

I found myself saying, "Actually I've just come from a country whose main party wants to do just that."

He looked incredulous: "Germany? Sweden? They take in a lot, but they don't make it an electoral promise."

"Scotland."

"Scotland? Where's that?" His expression was now perplexed and even slightly irritated, and after a pause, he said, "Isn't that part of England?"

"More or less, but they want to restore their independence."

"I know where you mean: mists, sheep and low mountains. Who would want to go up there anyway?"

Now I was strangely irritated. "You have to go there before you form an opinion."

"You're right," he conceded, as in our small town it's still bad manners to insist on contradicting your parents' friends. "They're not stupid, these Scots! They've understood that we need these people, because they remind us of who we were, of our better selves. We were all peasants once."

"Not all. Not Count Baracca over there!"

"No, but nearly all."

"True, but I don't know if they have it in them to return us to our former selves – always supposing that it's desirable."

"Of course it is," he countered with the certainty of youth.

"Maybe, but I agree that we have to rethink what borders are. They shouldn't be barriers, but merely the demarcation of jurisdictions. Everyone can cross them, but in so doing they accept the legal and cultural structure of the territory they have entered."[27]

I realised from that conversation that I was getting old, because I was beginning to find the young attractively different. Even their certainties can be noble in a way that ours – those of us older people – cannot.

By that time I had no intention of visiting my wife and child. Already it was something that suffused my body with dread, that sickly feeling of unpleasantness to come – unpleasantness that appears to be unavoidable, but it's all in the head. Nothing is inevitable, except for death, though that's not a thought that preoccupies me. The reality, in spite of my father's ravings, was that my visit would be as unpleasant for my wife as it would be for me. As for my daughter, she would look on this stranger with no more than vague curiosity and possibly with contempt. In fact, I was tired of pater, patron and patria. I felt that I never wanted to see them again. The most surprising thing was the rift with my fatherland, which I had always belonged to like I belong to my own skin. It remains within me, but I have no wish to experience it externally. This may be because the Italy within me is not the Italy of today, and if I'm to protect this Italy that is dear to me, I must never return to the Italy that is.

---

[27] Cinico appears to be very close to the beliefs of Immanuel Kant [translator's note]. I suppressed my desire to delete this superfluous note on De Oblivii's comment on the free movement of people, but we should remember that Cameron has no academic credentials [editor's note].

It occurred to me that only by staying abroad could I become myself – could I be free. That may sound like cowardice, and in a sense it is, but it's also a form of bravery. It's an experiment with free will.

What is a nation if not some form of oversized, abstract family? And usually dysfunctional. The Scots want so much to be a nation again, but the struggle to obtain independence may be more meaningful than the reality of it. At the time that these thoughts went through my head, I did not feel that I had to do something with my being abroad, beyond looking after my needs. I was right to think that I could do no good in Italy, but wrong to hanker only after comfort and my blessed anonymity.

IX

What Karim and the Estonian Had to Say

On my return to London and then Scotland, I had to go to Dundee to meet Maryanne and so I asked George to set up a few meetings. He was too busy to go, and I was in a good mood when I set off. The meetings were with dull technocrats who landed me with a mountain of statistics, some of it useful, at least in the journalistic sense. In the evening I went to see Maryanne who was at a trade-union office, a dusty room with chairs stacked against the wall, desks covered with disorderly papers and a quantity of ageing hardware – computers, printers, scanners and the like. There were five other campaigners and she quickly nodded that I should sit down on a chair some distance from them and immediately returned to a heated argument, which seemed interminable and not a little repetitive. Then came a string of words that stood out in bold, said by an elderly man who appeared to hold sway: "The problem is that we have absolutely no presence in the foreign press."

Perhaps because I was feeling neglected and perhaps because I had been rethinking my views on the referendum during my stay in Italy, I immediately grasped this opportunity to put myself centre stage and relieve the besieged independence supporters by riding to their rescue with the cohorts of *Il Messaggio del Popolo*, over which I had very little influence, but that felt like a quibble at the time. I rose and said in my sonorous voice, "I could write a long article in favour of Scottish independence, if you're interested in the Italian press. I could certainly get three thousand words into my paper, which would cover most of the main points."

And I then added vaguely and inaccurately, "And I have influential contacts."

The middle-aged man looked less than impressed, but Maryanne was transformed. "Could you, Cinico? Could you really?" she said and turned to her comrades, "He's a journalist with *Il Messaggio del Popolo*, based in Rome, and he comes up to Scotland regularly to cover the referendum." No one had heard of the newspaper, but a couple of them looked interested. Someone said, "How does that compare with *Corriere della Sera?*"

I had rushed on to the dance floor and now I had to dance.

The middle-aged man stood up and said that he had to go. He talked briefly about the need to involve the SNP. "Sometimes you have to," he said. The party had contacts in the European Parliament, in Brussels and elsewhere. He seemed to know his stuff, and also knew a bullshitter when he saw one. The others were less interested in his practicalities now they had a real-life foreign journalist willing and ready to go.

Of course, I was not expecting to be put to work immediately. Even for my employer, who pays me handsomely or at least the going rate, I would not dream of such a thing, but these dreamers of a better humanity work for free and work with passion. When I objected, not without a hint of petulance, that I had had no supper, they merely smiled and said that neither had they. It would not take long, they reassured me, and there too they were mistaken.

I had expected to get a pat on the back and the chance to leave with Maryanne; then later I would have concocted something akin to the content of the many campaign events I had frequented. That was not their interpretation; they were going to write the piece and I was merely going to be the translator. Improbably they were going to speak to the world through the columns of *Il Messaggio del Popolo*, a centrist paper with few ambitions, if there ever was one.

They were not driven by naivety, because if you asked them they would have expressed their own doubts. No, they were driven by something more admirable, more elusive and more foolish, which could only be defined as an excess of energy, a determination, a desire to leave no stone unturned, as though they feared that without this sacrifice they would forever reproach themselves for having failed in their enterprise on the 18th of September, with those terrible doubts, those ifs: if only we had done this, we could have done that.

Moreover, I was entirely redundant in this exercise, as they were better versed in the arguments than I was – by a long way. I had to wait in the company of my boredom and my hunger, the twin horsemen of the apparat. The first is never far away, and the second can be caused by the slightest shift in one's dietary routine. I was not in a happy mood, but was also unaware of the catastrophe I had now made inevitable, though inevitable it may have been already.

Eventually, the text was ready and they passed it to me excitedly. I looked at it, and it was as dense as it was formless. Illegible, mainly because it was too full of political jargon. Even in Italy, where people have good digestion when it comes to political prose, this was going too far and saying too much. But I pride myself on my ability to render the illegible legible. Hadn't I been doing it for creepy politicians since my mid twenties? Surely I could do it for these generous souls, which of course they were, in spite of their having obstructed my way to a plate of hot food. Apart from the first paragraph, I didn't read their article or rant there and then, but stared at it for what I thought was an appropriate time and said, "Excellent, that'll do nicely." I would have sold a kingdom for the chance to get out of that room, and they smiled, proud of their work.

At half past ten in the evening it is difficult to find food in a British provincial city, and in the end we had beer and crisps, which went down nicely with everyone else.

Maryanne and I went back to my hotel, and in the morning when I woke she was gone. Something had already changed, but not all for the worse. Change is as ambiguous as it is unpredictable; it gives and it takes away, and it enlivens the senses just as it deprives them. At least that is what I think now, though it wasn't what I thought at the time.

The vicissitudes of my trip to Italy had undoubtedly unsettled me, and my mood was so different from the heady days that preceded it. I went down to breakfast and even felt the absence of the good professor.[28] For some reason, my aloneness weighed on me, while I would usually find such moments restorative. I was suddenly aware of and disturbed by the postiche luxury that had surrounded so much of my life since I started work at the newspaper. I experienced the discomfort of comfort for the first time: its ubiquity, its lack of authenticity. The leftish disregard for the shabby paraphernalia of wealth no longer seemed so strange. I wasn't wholly converted. By no means, and perhaps I never will be. That was a moment of exquisite solitude. I belonged to neither camp, but I now knew where my greatest sympathies lay.

When I was at school, there was a lanky boy with a spotty face and a quizzical look who was obsessed with sex, even by the standards of our teenage years. His obsession appeared to be more intellectual than sensual, though it was possibly both, and I think of him now as a laboratory scientist passionately studying the mating habits of invertebrates. He often asked us the question, "Which is more important in sex, performance or patter?" His concern may have been

---

[28] "felt the absence": for some reason Cameron has translated literally from the Italian, *sentivo la mancanza del buon professore*, when he could have simply translated "even missed the good professor". After some discussion we decided to leave his version [editor's note].

personal as his conversation was only amusing to us boys, for he made the girls shudder. They didn't protest; they fled. At the time, I despised him, but now I feel pity for him and all teenagers, boys and girls, faced with a greater level of unknowability than we encounter at any other stage in life. I even feel some guilt about the boy, as his was an honest sleaziness, while mine has been a series of masks. I had the patter and benefitted from it not only in sexual matters.

But that particular question of his comes to mind now that I try to understand the Scottish referendum. It occurs to me that his approach should have been more logical: if patter is in any way significant – and it must be in some cases – then it has to be the more important, as a necessary first has to be in relation to a necessary second stage. And this has to be true of nations too. They are seduced by the powerful – whether they be monarchs, emperors, theocrats, plutocrats or elected politicians. We subject ourselves to them because of their promises, their patter, their charm, their pantomime and occasionally their sincere fantasies. We do so always on the basis of insufficient evidence or guarantees, and once we have entered into the relationship, we have to live with it and adapt to it.

The "we" that is a nation is far more irrational than the woman or man that a woman or man is trying to seduce. The nation works at the level of the crowd, the mass, and usually the instinct to conform in the absence of genuine dialogue. Where is the sane individual who would opt for war? But nations do this all the time. Individuals shudder and quite rationally fear for themselves and their loved ones, whilst the nation is titillated, energised, emboldened by an ill-defined glory that could touch everyone – a mirage they are drawn to like senseless automata.

Surely the nation is not an attractive thing. If it splits, is it improved? Does it only learn in defeat, when its newly acquired intelligence will be of little use?

But why stop at the nation? Haven't all our relationships become ones of seduction and transaction: of persuading somebody that something – even ourselves – is worth much more than something else and that something else – even our closest friends and relations – is worth much less. The nation may be declining in importance, not necessarily because we're more enlightened but because we believe in little beyond ourselves. The individual may be better than the group or the crowd, but this is not an argument for individualism. Individuals are only better when they act honestly and responsibly to others.

Most of these Yes campaigners are not primarily motivated by nationalism, but out of a sense of responsibility towards the victims of Scotland's despoliation through deindustrialisation, and also beyond the nation's borders – meaning a welcome to immigrants and concern for a just and fairer world. Of course, it'll fall short, but these revolutionaries fight with placards and leaflets, and not with violence. Surely they don't deserve the press they're given and the rhetoric of the Unionist parties.

I went up to my room to start on the translation, although the priority was an article on the increasing tensions in the ruling coalition of Conservatives and Lib-Dems. As I read through their work, it seemed better than it had the previous evening. No doubt a good breakfast had put me in a less belligerent mood, or perhaps it was my melancholy. Their article was too dense, but it was humane and it was hopeful. It contained an honest wisdom that no cynic should sneer at. I got down to work.

By the late afternoon I had finished both the translation and the article on the coalition, and therefore felt that I had done more than a day's work, and was a little disturbed to find that I was still on my own. I had not heard a word from Maryanne, and I thought it a bad policy to ring her. I started to read an Italian novel, something I rarely do and shortly afterwards gave up as it bored me. I padded around the hotel bedroom and for the want of something to do I decided to send off the translation without Maryanne's say-so. It also seemed a good idea because I had cut it quite a bit and changed the tone, though all the substance was there. Would she acknowledge that? Perhaps not, and so increasingly sensitive to her moods, I decided that I would copy her in.

Still time weighed on me like an imminent thunderstorm, fraying my nerves and setting my thoughts in a pointlessly circular motion. I had to leave the hotel for the first time in the day solely for something to do. I like wandering through strange cities on my own, but this time it was not pleasant. More than melancholy, I felt that my self-confidence was crumbling. I wandered into a poor area with quite a few immigrants and as I came round a corner and entered a lane I saw two men attacking another. I shouted and the two men fled, much to my surprise and relief as they were burly. I ran up to the man who had got up from the ground and looked shaken, but not angry.

"Did they take anything?" I asked.

"No, they did not. It is because I have not paid my rent." There was something very matter of fact about this reply, which he articulated in laboured English.

When I suggested that he go to the police, he laughed. When I offered to accompany him home, he rejected the offer. When I insisted, he said that he only would if I stayed for supper. He wanted me to meet his wife. I knew that hospitality is at the absolute centre of Arab culture – it was clear from his accent that he was Arab – and so I accepted, having already decided how I was to resolve the matter. Karim, as he revealed himself to be, explained on the way that he had escaped his village which had been under constant attack from the army in the nineties, but his situation was complicated by the fact he didn't agree with the religious leaders either. There seemed to be no room for someone like him during the conflict and he went abroad, as each side thought he supported the other. Nuanced ideas have no place in civil war. He didn't want to live in France and therefore travelled widely in Europe, often where no Algerian community existed. And he did a great variety of jobs. He met his North Korean wife while harvesting mussels on an English beach, but then the work was no longer available following a tragic drowning when the tide came in quicker than expected. By the time we got to his home, we were speaking in French, which turned out to be easier.

Inside the home, such as it was, his wife busied around preparing the supper, while he obviously enjoyed being hospitable in spite of the meagre ingredients to the meal, most of which were given to me. His wife spoke to me in an English that was worse than his, and I was able to elicit from her that they were six hundred pounds in arrears on their rent. The building was damp, and the paper on one wall was peeling. The furniture looked as though it had been rescued from a skip. They both worked long hours. They were childless and were too late for it now, and they were living a precarious life that the hardiest of students would reject even as a temporary solution.

I looked at them more carefully: he had a handsome, pre-maturely aged face – a sensitive man striving to survive each day, whilst she expressed a great resilience in spite of her studied deference to him. She deferred but he depended. I felt that he was determined to attain certain standards without which he would lose not just his dignity but also his essence as a civilised man. And it was not easy. She was more practical and where compromises were required, she made them. Sometimes we cannot afford our virtues, and she sacrificed hers for his.

At one point they moved into the small bedroom, the only other room in the flat except a tiny shower room. I heard them talking quickly in a language I couldn't recognise. I had to satisfy my curiosity, "What's the language you and your wife speak in?"

Suddenly he went very silent and looked questioningly at his wife, as though in search of assistance.

She looked up and said in a firm quiet voice with the polite hint of a smile East Asian women often adopt, "English. English."

"It only common language he speak I speak," she added by way of an apologetic explanation.

Then I was the one who was apologetic. Their words had been impenetrable, but neither did they suggest Arabic or Korean. That insane curiosity of mine had gone where there was no reason to go. I sensed in that moment their total isolation and their total interdependence. All that can be provided by humanity had to be provided by the other. I sensed how there's a world out there in turmoil. Vast numbers of people are shifting hopelessly around the world driven by wars or just the economic injustices of a system out of control. Desperate and exposed, people enter into apparently hopeless liaisons and yet such are their psychological resources they overcome the huge barrier to companionship and the cultural abyss they have to cross, and achieve relationships, however doomed, more significant than those of average couples less abandoned than they. This is the opposite of the seemingly adventurous and cosseted cosmopolitanism I enjoy. And within this maelstrom of migration, the most likely survivors are probably those who cling to their own, and that is why they will pay any price to join the company of relations or at least compatriots. But some are lost in the fearful tempests of change and find themselves utterly alone and unprotected.

These people – from the most maligned of tribes, those who flee poverty, famine, war, brutal regimes and murderous crowds – have greater humanity, not because they're all naturally more empathetic, but because they have learned to judge other humans intelligently and rationally by their acts and not by the mere signals of their animal presence, as we lazier and more pampered fellow beings often do. They learned this because they had to. Their lives depended on it.

In truth, we all learn from our misfortunes, but no one would wish to go through the terrors and calamities these people have suffered. They're better than us, and the shadow of their experiences will always darken their lives, even if they become wealthy and secure, and unlearn the real lessons of their experiences.

Of course there will be amongst them a few psychopaths, spies and fanatics fleeing their own crimes, but these, inflated into nightmares by the press, are but a tiny minority, whilst most turn towards submissiveness and gratitude. Yet we should be grateful to them, as they bring their skills and honest desire to contribute to the strange land they struggle to see as theirs. A nation, if nationalism is to have a positive meaning in the twenty-first century, must embrace these strangers who emerge from a night often provoked by the most powerful nations of the world. Sometimes their presence is uncomfortable, because they live with their emotions barely hidden under their skin, while we slumber in a surfeit of comfort and hang a "Do not disturb" sign from our sensitive noses.

These are people, I thought, whom we should listen to and learn from. They come from afar and they come from the past. We cannot save the Africans sold into slavery and transported as mistreated merchandise across an ocean, and we cannot save the Jews and Gypsies massacred through a bureaucratic-industrial machine fuelled by racism, but we can save this motley exodus. What sense is there in solemnly marking with ceremonial the cruelties that occurred decades or centuries ago, whilst ignoring those that occur today, or worse, finally acknowledging them and then failing to act decisively. We fear the messiness of today, while walking thoughtfully through the horrors of the past, which we have ordered and sanitised with simple narrative – our history is often more war cemetery than battlefield, more glory than horror. We should understand the present through the past, but to do so we also need to understand the past through the present. We ask ourselves how people could have allowed such terrible acts to take place, but surely we only have to look at the current increase in xenophobia and our fearful desire to sustain unsustainable standards of living to see how those acts could come about and understand how blindness can produce evil in us all. Or rather to understand the forceful presence of those things because in themselves they are never fully understandable.

I said that I had to get something from the car, although I didn't have a car, and that I would be back soon. I rushed to the nearest cash dispenser and used two cards to lift a thousand pounds, and then I rushed back. He resisted as I tried to stuff the money into his hand, but she plainly understood that pride was not a luxury they could afford. In the end he took it. She hugged me and said, "You good man," and he smiled stupidly, unable to understand.

He was not the only one. I had done something that I could never have imagined doing. I had given away a large sum of money to people I'd never met before. I thought that it would make me feel better, but it didn't. Was it too much? Or was it, more likely, too little? All I had done was arrange a stay of execution. This made me feel impotent, as well as slightly embarrassed with myself. I was behaving strangely.

The next day, Maryanne rang me and apologised for ignoring me. She thanked me for the translated article and wanted to know when it would be published. I couldn't say: it was an opinion piece, after all. Soon, I hoped.

"I've met this Estonian guy. He looks weird but has great ideas. You should meet him." She was as ever: vivacious, unbending, focused and ultimately someone who appeared to be enjoying life. "I'll stay tonight. You're off to London tomorrow, I think." "That's right." "Let's meet at the usual restaurant at eight o'clock. I'll invite the Estonian; he's called Jaan by the way." And she was gone. My hope was renewed, but exactly what I was hoping for, I could not say.

Shortly after her call, I got another less pleasant one from the editor. "What the fuck are you playing at?"

"What do you mean?"

"Your article."

"What about it?"

"Did you write it?"

"Of course."

"Have you gone mad? None of our readers want that stuff. Did you think you were writing for *Teoria Politica*?"[29]

"Of course not."

"Well, get it sorted. Here people associate the Scottish referendum with Lega Nord, because they're the only secessionists we've got. Mind you, I don't want you going off on a diatribe against the Lega either, because many of our readers vote for them. Do your usual thing: don't criticise or compliment anyone too much. Appear detached and urbane, above it all. And most importantly, keep it simple!"

"But it isn't like the Lega Nord ..."

"That may well be the case, Cinico, but it had better be like the Lega Nord in the new version you're going to write, or you'll be recalled to Rome and your cushy lifestyle will be over. Do you understand?"

I did. Only too well, and I spent the rest of the day rewriting a very different comment piece on the referendum.

When I got to the restaurant, Maryanne was already there, and sitting next to a man who could only be Jaan the Estonian. He was of average height, but gave the impression

---

[29] *Teoria Politica*: a multilingual yearly magazine of the left.

of being taller and was heavily built. He had a ponytail and wore a black imitation-leather jacket, but most extraordinary, he had grown a goatee of prodigious length – around ten centimetres. Because he was in the habit of resting his chin on his right hand, his goatee often veered to the left as though it were giving directions. He clearly didn't give a damn, though occasionally he would grasp it and stroke it gently and thoughtfully until it adopted a more sensible downward direction.

When he spoke, he was animated: his eyes would bulge, his lids wink, his mouth grin, and his lips curl, twist or open to roar or laugh. I don't think he was typical of Estonians, generally a reserved people, but then I don't think he was typical of anywhere.

"This is Jaan and he speaks five languages: English, Russian, Finnish, Swedish and of course his own language, Estonian," she said expansively. They had both stood up, which I found a little formal, as though I were the outsider.

I looked at him with as much detachment as I could muster, and shook his hand. He looked embarrassed about the introduction, and tried to dilute it by saying, "My Swedish is not that fluent."

"He's been through this before; he was a teenager when Estonia broke free of the Soviet Union," she continued to effuse.

"The situation was quite different. Scotland is motivated by where it wants to go, while Estonia was motivated by where it wanted to get away from," he countered.

Sometimes you can tire of politics, but I'm not sure that these people could. I grinned, as I thought that something was required of me.

"Well, at least Estonia has done it. It's free now and can get on with its own business," I said while my conscience started to scream at me. Had I been too hasty in my meek response to the editor? "Let's hope that Scotland is as successful." She may have thought that I sounded insincere, but he took the statement at face value and as an excuse to expatiate on the whole matter in its global context:

"There's a narrow lane in Tallinn on which the council has inlaid in brass Estonia's past and future; it ends unwisely with 2418, being the 500th anniversary of the Estonian Republic. Unwise because it's foolish to tempt fate with such predictions, even when, as in this case, they are entirely benign and to be hoped for. I am only too aware of how war, famine and other cataclysms can sweep small countries away – and even the big.

"The council's big-hearted prophecy is a Ruritanian, naive and quite understandable version of Hitler's malign thousand-year Reich, which lasted only twelve. It lacks the latter's megalomania, and what it gains in modesty it loses in realism. It is not so much a spell as a soporific. We won't find longevity amongst the many advantages of being a small country, whilst one of the most important ones is that small countries have to be clever. In English you say 'box clever', but the metaphor is no longer a happy one, because the cleverness of a small nation can never again be a boxer's aggression – that is a military advantage which was sometimes possible when weaponry was less sophisticated. Athens could no longer stand up to the Persian Empire or the early Swiss cantons to the Hapsburgs. For the small country to survive today, it has to be educated, very educated, and it has to be open to the world. This is not easy and so the nation can never relax. This may sound exhausting but it isn't. Not at all. It's exhilarating. Excessive comfort is exhausting because the soul goes to sleep and experiences almost nothing. The big nation is a sloth, and a small nation is a nervous deer, always awake to the next danger. Its people must constantly maintain the dykes and keep the sea at bay – and those dykes are its own culture and intelligence, but not its ethnic purity.

"A small nation should not fear immigration, but often

it will. This is one of the small nation's most common mistakes. Holland made itself great through immigration and then provincial through its recent xenophobia. It is the small nation's task to keep its language and culture alive – 'task' is too small a word for this unrelenting and monumental striving. And the small country doesn't do this just for itself; it does it for the whole planet which is itself a living organism that survives through the variety of its biological species and one particular species's nations, languages, cultures, individual strivings and happenchance.

"In Estonia, many people fear immigration, whereas emigration is the danger. Immigrants send their children to school where they learn the national language. They represent no danger at all to the national culture; they strengthen it and even add to it. Emigration has taken away our young people, our learning, our investment in learning. The greatest threat to our culture is, however, the English language, which is fast becoming the lingua franca of Europe. It's not even native English speakers we have to fear, it is the ubiquity of the language, in a world where we can travel so easily and so quickly. Soon Latvians and Estonians will communicate in English, and then within the open borders of Europe English will gradually become too dominant, first contaminating our languages and then replacing them. This may seem far off, but the Estonians haven't even perceived the danger, and are obsessed with fighting the Russians, who now only want to protect their own very long and exposed borders.

"Linguistically, Scotland and Ireland aren't really small countries, as they speak the dominant language. To speak only the dominant language is to think only like the dominant power. To become a real small country, Scotland has to revive Gaelic and Scots. Keep English please; it's the key to the global world, but become polyglot like us. Small countries are polyglot by nature, and it allows them to see the world in many different ways."

The Estonian could certainly talk, and he didn't even seem out of breath.

"You see what I mean," Maryanne said, "he just keeps going. We should get him to write an article for *Il Messaggio del Popolo*, and you could translate it."

Whilst her effusion made Jaan look uncomfortable, her mention of the newspaper put me into a panic. I could barely focus, and the sense that nothing in my life was under my control became overpowering.

The Estonian, sensing that more was happening at the table than he could comprehend – or maybe not – decided to continue with his lecture, and this did give me some respite.

"Estonians and Latvians have treated their Russian minorities badly and this was a mistake. Like immigrants, they could have been integrated, but they were purposefully alienated. Many don't have a vote and don't have a proper passport. The two communities live separately, and encase the other in negative stereotypes: this is not wise for a small nation. But these are not immigrants; some of the Russian families are in their third generation in Estonia and Latvia. Both communities have lost a lot of their young people, and often the most educated ones."

"So you don't hate Russians, but you hated the Soviet Union," I decided to work my way into the conversation.

"I don't hate anyone. And I wanted independence of Estonia, because it is a nation. I am a communist – Marxist, if you like – but was critical of the Soviet Union because it thought it could create socialism through annexation. This doesn't work, as history has shown. It's counterproductive – and it's wrong. The Soviet Union was stultifying, stupid and badly led, but it had its positive sides too, as many have had to admit. Good healthcare and education, and full employment. The producer and not the consumer was held in consideration, and I'm for that. Besides if I dislike anybody, it's those who rise to the top in any regime.

Many of those who collaborated with the Russians, now sing the praises of Nato. Those who opposed them as dissidents in the Soviet Union, now talk of social rights and sometimes mix with the Russians. There is no left to speak of, but there is an awareness amongst some ex-dissidents that the market cannot resolve every problem. And that makes them dissidents again. They have integrity but no power, and then there are those who have power and yet cannot even be defined as compromised, because they have no principles to compromise. The smell that comes off them is immediately recognisable, and you can smell it in your democracies too."

I asked no more questions, as the man was exhausting me. You pressed a button and out came the appropriate spiel. He had it all worked out in his head. I turned to Maryanne and started to talk small, about the good professor, the newspaper, the events she had spoken at, and Jaan politely listened – as relaxed in his silence as he had been in his loquacity. However, his last comments reminded me of the story of an elderly schoolteacher of mine. When Lugo was liberated by a turbaned and kilted army of Indians of the 1st Jaipur Infantry and Scottish Highlanders in April 1945, the Committee of National Liberation set up its new local government. At the time, the schoolteacher lived in San Lorenzo, a small township just five kilometres from Lugo. As it was a working-class district, only the Communists, Socialists and Republicans were represented on the committee, and shortly afterwards one of the representatives visited the schoolteacher, who had fought with the communist partisans, and asked or rather commanded him to act as the secretary and keep the minutes of their proceedings. He agreed on condition that he would be released from his duties once they had found a suitable substitute. At the first meeting, held in the modest and bomb-damaged town hall, he discovered that all the representatives were similar men in plain suits:

lawyers, doctors, teachers and owners of some of the few businesses San Lorenzo could boast. Many were closely related and often across party lines.

The first to speak was an ageing Republican, a tall man of almost patrician demeanour who spoke a lugubrious and grandiloquent Italian and declared that he alone had never been enrolled in the Fascist Party and would like to know why the others had been. The consternation of the representatives of the new regime could not be avoided. One by one they had to stand up and explain their reasons for stooping so low and compromising themselves with the dictatorship, and those of us who haven't lived in such political systems shouldn't sneer at them.[30] Each one drank their full portion of humiliation until they arrived at the last speaker, an affable and jocular socialist and businessman who frequented everyone and whose exact business activities were known to no one.

He stood up slowly and with a smile said, "I have no intention of discussing or excusing my Fascist party card; under Mussolini no one could get on without one and no one could have known how long he would last. We weren't fools and we understood how the world works. I'm surprised by our Republican colleague's claim, because I was on the Fascist committee that vetted all applications for party membership in this part of Romagna, and I was the one who spoke decisively against his application. If he was never in the Fascist party, the merit is all mine."

Apparently there was some disorder in the council chamber following this revelation, which proved little more than the impossible murkiness of the political world. How can we avoid cynicism in the knowledge of such things? Shortly afterwards, the teacher found a replacement secretary. That man went on to a great local career and became mayor of

---

[30] Actually our regimes also punish dissidence, but more subtly and more selectively [author's note].

one of our larger rural towns; his predecessor lived out the rest of his life as a humble secondary-school teacher, the first to abandon the *zappa*[31] and follow a professional career with all the purposefulness and measured egalitarianism of his peasant roots. That was probably as it should have been; everyone should follow their own nature, while perhaps trying to improve it gently.

As we walked back to my hotel, I said to her, "You've got quite a thing about that Estonian. Maybe I should be jealous."

Irritatingly she pinched my cheek and shook it, "Don't be silly. Did you take a good look at him? Don't tell me my Latin lover[32] is feeling insecure."

We're all insecure. It's the human condition, but no one likes it to be pointed out because, for our own psychological health, we refuse even to admit it to ourselves. Perhaps when we're old and tired, insecurity will matter less. But when our lives are still to be made, the goddess of fortune rather than Medusa is the one that turns us to stone, should we be so foolish as to look her in the face.

But her words made me feel a little more secure and soothed my irritation. I even started to like the Estonian, who was interesting as well unusual. His hair – both facial and cranial – was a metaphor for his nature and beliefs. He could be pulled in both directions. A nationalist and an internationalist, a communist who criticised the Soviet Union, an Estonian speaker who sympathised

---

[31] *zappa*: a large, broad hoe also used for digging, which to some extent symbolises the Italian peasantry.

[32] "Latin lover": in English in the original, because this was a common Anglicism in Italy during the sixties and seventies, and then began to fade out from the late seventies as the feminist movement began to assert itself. It's unlikely that Maryanne could have known the expression unless Cinico had previously used it. Another example of his old-fogeyness.

with the Russian speakers in Estonia, a European convinced that Europeans are going mad with xenophobia,
an advocate of the Estonian language and culture more
fearful of American culture than of the Russian, he was,
I think, a man who had a good heart, but was as ugly as
sin. I could relax.

X

What the Swede So Persuasively Didn't Have to Say

When we rose the next morning, I was in an excellent
mood, and beginning to convince myself that I cared
about the Scottish referendum – and to some extent I
did. We went down to an extended breakfast and chat-
ted happily, and all the time the problem of the translated article and its non-appearance in the newspaper
was repressed into the remotest part of my unconscious.
If it came anywhere near to my conscious mind, it was to
reassure me that she would probably never find out, demonstrating how little I knew about obsessives. Eventually
Maryanne had to leave and I wandered around the foyer
for a bit before going to my room to pack. I was in no
hurry to catch the train for London.

The man at the reception, whom I now knew quite well,
called me over and told me that I wasn't the only foreign
journalist there. There was a Swedish one reading his paper
in the corner. I may have wanted to speak to him, he suggested, and for some reason I immediately thought that this
was a good idea.

I walked over to the Swede, possibly even with a bit of
a swagger, and announced myself to be a journalist with *Il
Messaggio del Popolo*, which he may well never have heard of,
but didn't reveal himself either way. I started to talk about
the referendum in a very expert manner, and after a while,
I realised that I was expounding all the arguments in the
translated article that wouldn't be published. All the time
he was holding the paper up ready to return to his reading at
the first chance. So far he had not said a word. I paused and
looked at him enquiringly – was he going to cut me dead?

"You may well be right," he said at last, and then lifted his paper fully up to reading level and returned to it. That might well have been the end of the conversation, had fate not intervened in the shape of a kink in the paper. He had to postpone his reading a little further while he shook the paper to flatten it out, and during that brief interval he must have pondered his response and found the single sentence to be incomplete. He added the missing part: "though I would reflect on it a little longer, if I were you."

XI

What Maryanne, the Lithuanian, the Leader of the Allotment Society and the German All Had to Say

I went to Edinburgh and then took the east coast train down through England. Halfway there you enter the flatlands of Eastern England, which resemble those of the Po Valley for their wide horizons and intensive agriculture, but they aren't as fertile, just as they are more fertile than anywhere in Scotland. I felt that I was returning to the centre of Western Europe where people believe that they're better off, though possibly aren't. I was going back to a supposedly comfortable and stimulating lifestyle, which many would envy – which many would give their right arm to have. And so it had been, but what had been comfortable no longer felt so, and what had been stimulating had lost all intellectual attraction. With each mile I felt emptier and with each mile I felt safer. I had a choice to make.

By the time I got to King's Cross, the problem of the translated article appeared to have resolved itself. Different challenges awaited, and to some extent I looked forward to my old life.

For two weeks I failed to get in contact with my lover which, looking back, was an odd thing to do in the circumstances. In part, there was a lot on and I was doing something that came easily: sometimes we need that. But it was also my fear that she would plague me with questions about their document whose publication they awaited with an eagerness that bordered on the insane – an insanity not devoid of a healthy belief in humanity's potential goodness.

If I had a guilty conscience, it was hidden in my unconscious – clearly my better half.

Then, while I was at work at the hot desk the newspaper paid for, she rang and said without any reference to middle-class etiquette, "You absolute cunt, you!" I restrained my flippant nature that wanted to point out that pleonasms are not usually considered good grammar in any language, and though I was not yet unduly concerned, I knew what it was about. What I had feared would happen was now happening and strangely this came as a relief. I was almost jaunty.

I compounded all my errors by failing to start with the extenuating circumstances: namely the fact that my job was at risk. Instead I said with inexcusable glibness, "How did you find out?"

Then, the floodgates opened and the bile flowed out: "Arrogant bastard, you don't even try to sweet-talk your way out. How did I find out? Who cares, you bastard? It's the finding out that matters to you, not what you do. You utter sleazebag!"

"Hold on, Maryanne, you don't have to be so offensive. I have feelings, you know," I said in a louder voice, genuinely overcome by the fierceness of the assassination.

"Like a snake, you mean! Oh and if you want to know how I found out: it turns out that Jaan is also pretty fluent in Italian and he translated the two very different versions – the one you sent me and the one in the paper."

"Maryanne, you've no right …"

"Every right."

"Why are you making such a fuss about a single article written in a foreign language to be read by people who've more on their minds than a Scottish referendum? They're not that interested in their own."

"You don't understand. We don't deal with hundreds of thousands, we get to hundreds of thousands by building up fives and tens – getting everyone involved and speaking in small groups. It's not the school-hall meetings that are the primary force in our campaign – though they are impor- tant – it's the small encounters up and down the country. Sometimes they're just one-to-one. We don't have the media at home, and if we can at least neutralise some of the non- sense they're talking about us abroad, then that's another tiny step. I never had great expectations of your article, but I didn't think that you would go over to the other side."

"You wanted me to throw up my career for an article?"

"Why not?" she breathed hoarsely down into her phone.

"I'm more practical than you, and my question even shorter: why?"

"Do I have to spell it out? If you were a man, you'd act according to your conscience and the promises you freely made. I never forced them on you; you volunteered, remember?"

"You're talking about my career? If I want to leave the paper, I'll find another job first."

"You couldn't force them to print your original article, but you didn't have to write what they wanted, whoever they are. What did you have to lose?"

"My job! I keep telling you, my job was on the line."

"I doubt it. They might have recalled you back to the coalface you're trying to avoid. In the meantime, you've lost something else."

"Like what?" I asked expecting the answer to be her.

"Your soul."

"Means nothing to me. I'm not that metaphysical, and even if I were, I would have to admit that I sold it to the devil long before now."

"Okay, in that case, your balls, and I'm speaking to man who is particularly proud of his genitalia."

"You're just a fanatic, and we paid a high enough price for them in the twentieth century; God protect us from them in the twenty-first."

I was riled and wanted to provoke her, but to my surprise,

she simply said, "That's your opinion, and you're welcome to it," and the phone went dead.

Looking up I could see that some of my fellow lone wolves of the newspaper world were looking at me and others were smiling as they typed. She was right to be angry with me: that was my first thought. I had looked on them as naive to want so much for this article published in a middle-ranking Italian newspaper with a depleting readership little interested in them and their struggle. But they knew that. The importance they attached to it was motivated by their frustration over newspapers in general. Apart from the weekly *Sunday Herald*, they had no platform in the traditional media. Nearly all of the foreign press followed the lead of the national papers. The No campaign mainly exploited the electorate's understandable fears of the unknown, though of course all futures are unknown, and it was also very personal in its attacks and coordinated across the media. Back in February the governor of the Bank of England had visited the Scottish First Minister, and the newspapers led with victory cries for the No campaign: "Carney in Currency Warning to Scotland" in the FT, "Don't Bank on It" in the *Daily Mail*, and "Bank's Pound Threat to Nats". Through the alliterations and puns of Britain's elliptic headlines you can sense the contempt for those outside the press's palisade. Yet when the No's strategists got their polling results they were surprised to find that the Yes campaign had won that particular encounter. It seemed that people were losing faith in traditional media.

The Yes campaign was winning the online battle, but its exclusion from the papers and to a slightly lesser extent from the TV and radio rankled. Those valid arguments in the translated letter deserved a wider audience in a genuinely democratic debate. They could be heard, but only by those who went out to look for them: online or by going out in the evening to a local event. They had to be active and many were. Then there was also canvassing, which is the habit of going door to door, something unknown to us in Italy. This was another area in which Yes excelled, and was driven by energetic and usually youthful supporters. What Maryanne and her fellow campaigners wanted was at least a small breech in the media Berlin Wall.

It would have been pointless calling her back. I had to get the next train to Scotland without notifying the paper.

For two days I tried to contact her, but she was not contactable. I went to see George Lovenight in the hope of finding some story to justify my flight north. He too was of little use. Someone notified me of a rally in George Square at the centre of Glasgow. You come to the square as soon as you leave Queen Street Station. I had only to cross half the square to see Maryanne walking with the Estonian and she had her arm through his. In other words, he was where I should have been. I shouted her name and ran across. She turned and looked unbothered.

"Come to see the Scottish Lega Nord?"

"Maryanne!"

"How dare you compare us to those racist bastards in their absurd green uniforms. What you did was a huge betrayal – worse than sleeping with another woman, which I might have forgiven."

"That's ridiculous."

"Look, you can categorise humanity many different ways, but there's one you probably haven't thought of: the division between those who don't care about politics and those who do, who believe that nothing can be achieved without it. This is the first time the Scottish people have been consulted as a people, and we could do something really important for us, for Europe and maybe even for the world."

"You take a lot on for a small country."

"Precisely because it's a small country," she puffed her cheeks to express her difficulty in explaining this to me. "Small countries don't invade other ones. Small countries don't believe that they have all the answers, and should decide what governments other countries should have. Small countries have to work with other countries, big and small, and know their limitations. Sure, small countries can be smug, xenophobic, precious and even a bit kitsch about their own cultures. That's why we've got to do it differently. Can't you see that?"

"I can. I can now, I think. Jaan," I turned to him, "could you leave us on our own for a minute?" She looked uncertain, but he was already moving away and waved his arm to indicate that she should stay.

"What are you doing? Working round the entire European Union?" I said failing to suppress the desperation in my voice.

"No, the whole world," she laughed defiantly and then gave me one of those stares they have around those parts. They silently but effectively convey the more explicit order, "Get out of my face!" – another typically Scottish cordiality.

"But with him?" I tried again and almost pleadingly – a little weakly too, mainly because I couldn't understand her behaviour.

"I'm in love with his mind," she said.

"It must be a fantastic mind to make up for that body."

"Oh it is, I can assure you," she said cruelly. "And it's a pleasant change from you: a great body with the mind of a complete fuckwit."

She shifted the strap of her handbag over her shoulder and turned to walk away without another word or glance in my direction, making those words the last ones I would ever hear her say.

The reader may feel that I was a poor Don Giovanni to relinquish my loved one with so little of a fight; after all, I had plotted seductions more carefully in the past for women whose only attraction was their resistance and who ceased to attract once they had been conquered – once my curiosity had been sated, which in some cases was in a few days or even after a single night.

Personally I believe that I was affected by Northern European romanticism, which finds its purest form in Scotland. Some will laugh at such a distortion of obvious realities, but they would misunderstand what I mean by romanticism. Popular opinion holds Southern Europeans to be romantic, as they are freer with their emotions and less constrained by Christian sexual morality in its most hidebound form – generally referred to as Protestantism. But the romantic view of sex is precisely the product of that northern repressiveness. Southern Europeans and in particular Italians (both male and female) are more practical lovers, and care less about some romantic ideal, which in any case is disappearing fast along with the religions that sustained it.

My thinking – and this may be self-delusion – is that I relinquished Maryanne because I loved her and therefore had to respect her, and moreover I didn't want to sully our relationship with the inevitable compromises and disappointments of prolonged cohabitation.

Or perhaps – more simply and less romantically – I renounced the campaign because I knew it was already lost and her mind was made up – I was a coward fearful of the humiliations I could have encountered. I lost because of pusillanimity and not because of principle.

I took the train back to Edinburgh in a dark mood, but not without a light at the end of the tunnel or of the oncoming train.[33] If all things are turning against you, the best tactic may not be to take them all on at the same time, but as this wasn't a military campaign, what could go wrong? I would never know without at least having a try. Let Maryanne

---

[33] This play on one of the most common British clichés was quite fresh in the way Cinico used it in the original, but the return to its original language works less well.

climb on to her barricade and wave her saltire around, while Jaan looks on admiringly as his head is pulled in all sorts of wonderful directions. I would see the referendum through to its completion, and then move on to where others were in struggle, perhaps with more desperate and more terrible odds. After all, the Scots only have to vote for it. If they don't, do they deserve it?

I would think things out for the first time. I had refused to because I didn't want to turn into one of the dreamers of my parents' generation, but that's what happens: we turn into something vaguely similar to our parents by striving too much not to be like them. What I had realised is that some things matter: worse than morality, which I have always mistrusted, is amorality, and worse than amorality is moralising. Morality, at least, does not go beyond the borders of the self. It doesn't judge the behaviour of others who must be left to their own devices and their own moral strictures, for who can say which morality is right and which wrong? From now on I would live my life by my own lights.

I would do all this, if I could find the energy, which was unlikely in any person, but particularly in someone as cosseted as I had been.

By the time I got to my hotel, I felt that I was doing well at disentangling my life and my ideas, and I may have got further if I hadn't found George who had decided to visit. I knew then that it had been a mistake to contact him, and yet he was all I had. I'd cut myself off from everybody.

He stood up from the designer plastic chair in the foyer, grinned at me, and said, "Cinico, you look absolutely awful. What's happened to you? You need a rest." And he gave me a friendly pat on the back. I must have looked bad. Clearly my new-found decisiveness was not yet publicly visible.

"A long story, George. Another day, if you don't mind. What can I do for you?"

"What can I do for you, Cinico? You need cheering up."

"I think I need a shower and an afternoon nap."

"Cinico, I've got a much better idea. Why don't we go to lunch and then move on to the meeting of a very special upmarket allotment society?"

"I can think of several reasons why I wouldn't go for the after-lunch entertainment."

"Ah, but do you know who's the chairperson of this society?"

"No."

"Kurt Springfit!"

"And who's he?"

"Only the greatest political psephologist who ever lived." There followed an endless curriculum vitae which on another day might have impressed me. However, I allowed myself to be persuaded. This could be a distraction, I thought.

George took me to a small Italian trattoria – it was his choice and the food was surprisingly better than expected. When we'd finished eating, the manager came over to ask if we'd enjoyed our meal. She was a smart, efficient and attractive woman of around thirty years – the kind of person who would do well anywhere. As she was about to leave us, I asked where she was from: her slight accent that was difficult to place.

"Lithuania," she said.

"And do you like it here?" I asked.

"Of course, this is a beautiful city, and I have come to feel very much at home."

"You see," said the good professor, "this lady is exactly the kind of immigrant we want – one who wants to integrate and get on with the job."

"No, no," she responded with unexpected heat, "that's not what I mean at all. This was a decision that I made. I freely chose to take on this Scottish or British identity. Other people can make their own decision. You know, I

145

come from Vilnius which has one hundred and twenty-eight ethnicities within its city limits, and yet we all live together. Now sixty-three per cent of Vilnius's population is Lithuanian, the majority as you would expect. But you would be surprised to know this is not the other ethnicities coming to push the percentage down; it's the other way around, and it's the Lithuanians who have been steadily taking over since the war. Before the war, the Poles were the largest group followed by the Yiddish speakers, and there were hardly any Lithuanians within the boundaries of the ancient Lithuanian capital, which was actually part of Poland at the time. When the country became independent of the Soviet Union, Landsbergis gave citizenship to everyone living in the country. So you see, different cultures can live alongside each other and maintain their different cultures."

"Thank you for the history lesson, young lady," said George with a sour smile, "part of the service, I imagine. What you're suggesting may work in Lithuania but would never work here. Of course, we're very tolerant as I think most fair-minded foreigners would concede."

She smiled back at him with the blank smile of someone who is having to exercise a degree of patience. "I'm just saying that real integration can only occur if it's freely chosen and not forced. And there's no need to force it. Everywhere is changing all the time, even ethnically. Historically this may have been more dramatic in the country I come from, but it happens here too. It has too."

"Well, well," he said as he stood up and without looking at her, "you may be trying to integrate, but clearly you haven't quite managed it yet."

When we got to the allotments, I recognised Springfit from his TV appearances and also remembered some very misleading statistics on the comparative figures for Scotland and England on public attitudes to Trident, something

I've been aware of doing in my own work. It is part of the trade. Still I thought that Lovenight had exaggerated his CV, living as he did in his Scottish bubble. It could be said with only a little exaggeration that the No camp consisted of English imperialists and Little Scotlanders, proud to be Scottish and proud to be British, as though pride were a virtue rather than a form of stupidity or at least wilful self-delusion.

As it was a sunny day, the meeting took place on the lawn close to the clubhouse, because this was no flat-hat allotment society, but one of means. After various formalities, Springfit stood up amongst the four or five elite gardeners on the slightly raised wooden platform and walked to the microphone: "Fellow gardeners, today promises to be an interesting debate because we are faced with a crucial and now pressing issue: not only is Dr Singh's coriander crossing our agreed borders and invading the territory of other members of our esteemed society, but he has once again raised the fraught question of non-indigenous species, which we have been ignoring for far too long. My personal view and, I have to say, the view of all previous AGMs has been that only native Scottish species should be growing in our allotments. There's nothing intolerant about this, and I like coriander in my curry just as much as the next man. In fact, I have often advocated the health benefits of occasionally partaking of South Asian cuisine, and Mrs Springfit is very partial to chicken biryani." At this stage he chortled as though he had said something funny, and some of his fellow gardeners obliged by emitting bird-like twitters. "However, we need to defend the integrity of our Scottish flora from invasive foreign species, and coriander, which is particularly invasive, has drawn our attention to a wider problem.

"I think that Jim is especially aggrieved as he has one of the allotments bordering with Dr Singh's and has taken the brunt of the frontal attack."

Jim stood up and surveyed the meeting like a prosecutor

in a celebrity murder trial. Now was the chance to express all his pain to an understanding audience. "My cabbages have suffered, as have my carrots and Swiss chard, but what upsets me most is the complete annihilation of my peonies. They are my wife's favourite flower, and my wife, as many of you know, has not been well for many years."

Some of the gardeners clicked their tongues to express their suppressed compassion, while I wondered at the dangerously suspect Swiss interloper who only later I discovered to be our very own much-loved *bietola*.

"My peonies mean a lot to my wife, but when I complain to Dr Singh, he apologises and does absolutely nothing. When I complain again, he apologises and says he's very busy."

"He's a heart surgeon," someone objected.

"He may well be, but that gives him no right to invade my peonies."

"Thank you, Jim," the chairman interrupted, sensing that Jim was about to overplay the Peony Question, "you've put your argument cogently and we must now consider what we have to do."

"Hold on, chairman," someone shouted, "have we actually decided that there is a problem? It's not a problem for me, and my plot also borders with Dr Singh's. There's plenty of room for coriander in these allotments. In fact, I wish that his coriander had wandered over into my plot. Can't get enough of it."

"Look," said the chairman, now peeved, "this is not about personal preference. We have a duty to Scotland to protect our native species."

"But what do you mean by native species? The Romans brought a whole lot that are now considered native, as coriander will be in a hundred years time," came another voice.

"The Scots were never under the Romans."

"Yes they were. The Romans went as far as the Antonine Wall."

"Actually they went further and won the Battle of Mons

Graupius."

"This is nonsense! Nature doesn't respect land borders; if they brought something to Londinium, it would have worked its way north."

The chairman didn't look as though he was enjoying the interesting debate he had hoped for. He hammered the podium with his fist, and shouted, "Every year it's the same thing. Every year we fail to take action on this vital question." But no one listened. No one cared, which for me came as a relief. I got up to go.

For some reason the good professor came running after me. "Why are you leaving so soon? The best is to come, and you can meet Springfit when they have tea afterwards."

"Why would I want to do that?" I replied, also rebelling against the idea of tea as the British make it. You have to be born and brought up on this island to appreciate that drink. "Well indeed," I continued, picking up on a common British expression, "this is definitely not my cup of tea. I'm the first to admit that I have lived a frivolous life, but I have never dressed up my frivolity in so much grand rhetoric as these people do. I rarely adopt one side or the other in an argument, but in this case I don't even engage my brain. The proceedings were entertaining only because of their absurdity."

My words incensed George Lovenight, and this was immediately oppressive. I wanted to escape that foolishness. He gave me a lecture on how the middle classes worked for the good of all society and needed distractions to help them unwind. In this best of all possible worlds, the people most squeezed were the ones with the most responsibilities. Even my cursory tour of Scotland had shown that this is clearly not the case. This was the moment when I realised the full extent to which the political conflict I had been observing was one of class – particularly for people like George Lovenight and Jim Paterson who face each other across a deep divide affecting all of Europe and the world beyond.

He too had decided not to stay at the meeting, partly because we were both being drawn into an argument. As we walked back to his car and then on the drive back to the city centre, we managed to disagree on just about everything. "Your brain has turned to mush," he said, "since you started to sympathise with the Yes campaign. It's difficult to argue with you people, because your ideologies have no interest in the facts. It's infuriating, it's like whack-a-mole."

"They say the same of you, but they use examples, while 'you people' just assert."

"Clearly you've been hanging around that woman too much – you know, the dark-haired one I've seen you chatting to. She's a fanatic, you should have seen that straightaway when she gave you a hard time for no reason."

I didn't pursue the matter with him, as I too had called her a fanatic. Now I saw it differently: isn't there something that might be called "fanatical stasis" or "fanatical conservatism", which declines to admit to any reason beyond the maintenance of the status quo, even though hundreds of thousands of Scottish children are living under the poverty line, unemployment and underemployment are blighting the lives of great swathes of the adult population, services are deteriorating because the economic system makes it impossible to raise taxes from the rich, and the downward spiral in wages and working conditions means that little more can be squeezed out of the poor? Such fanatical ostriches fail to realise that this trajectory cannot go on forever, just as they failed to realise that you cannot go on offering mortgages to poorer and poorer people. Why should the person alert to the enormity of these problems and their irresolvability within the system be defined as a fanatic rather than a perfect rationalist? No one says that the solutions are easy to identify, and once they are, the transition is not going to be easy either. But that's no reason to turn your back fanatically on the hecatomb of useful lives burning out of sight.

The subject over which we argued most fiercely was

immigration. This was the issue that most attracted me to the Yes voters, their belief in not only treating asylum seekers humanely as required by international agreements, but also immigration itself. This desire not to be independent from the world but independent in the world was unusual in an independence movement, and justified Maryanne's anger at my associating them with the Lega Nord. Some went further: they saw what the world could do for Scotland and more importantly what Scotland could do for the world.

As we argued, I realised that the good professor wasn't really arguing for this being the best of all possible worlds, but rather for Britain being the best of all possible countries, and the world's role in this celestial order was to keep Britain in that primary position. In my opinion he had never understood the relative nature of foreignness: the idea that he was a foreigner to others – to me, for example – had never fully registered in his right-thinking mind. Readers of these notes, being Italians, will find this difficult to believe. For us, "foreigner" is not an insult; after all, we have a word for the love of all things foreign.[34] Because the one and a half centuries our youngish country has existed as a united state have been troubled and its underlying problems intractable, we look to other countries for guidance on one side or the other: to America or Russia, to France or Germany, and to Scandinavia or England. One of the strangest conceits of the English is that they're the only ones who laugh at themselves, and yet they laugh at peccadilloes (such as mad dogs and Englishmen going out in the noonday sun[35]) that

---

[34] *esterofilia* [translator's note]. English does in fact have the word, "xenophile", but its frequency of use is extremely low, and Italian also has the lesser-used *esteromania*, which suggests an excessive – possibly unmerited and irrational – love of things foreign [editor's note].

[35] Who knows where Cinico picked up this titbit from decades gone by? I cannot restrain myself from adding a comment my own:

they barely amount to self-criticism (more a boast of divine eccentricity), whilst we curse and laugh at ourselves for faults that strike at our very existence: our corruption, our vacillation, our ungovernability, when most of these things are far from exclusive to us – they may even be innate to the human condition.

I think that it's the island that makes the British think like this. Surrounded by water, an island state is never familiar with the foreign and being foreign. It has no borderlands, where people mix, influence each other, hate each other and grow like each other, thus blurring the line of demarcation that dominates their lives. Even a country like ours, which has water on three sides and borders on the fourth with five countries, knows how to mix, merge and reject.

Often Scots who supported the continuance of the union with England would say, "Am I supposed to think of the English as foreigners?" And in my head, I replied, "Why not? A foreigner is still a human being. Is nationality that important any more? Aren't Scotland's foreignness to England and England's foreignness to Scotland to be embraced as a novel form of brotherhood and contention? Particularly if both countries were to remain in the European Union. In fact, an independent Scotland may well bind England to the EU, as it's already showing signs of wanting to leave, but would think twice if reduced in size.[36]

It has become clear to me that we often take people for

---

these Englishmen were not all Englishmen but Englishmen wearing pith helmets, in other words imperial visitors and officials, ignoring the fact most of the middle and lower-ranking cadres of the British Empire were often Scots and Irish, particularly in the less salubrious postings. Of course pith helmets exclude women too, but clearly the English ladies would not be promenading at that time of day! Eccentricity was a male and upper-class occupation.

[36] This idea of Cinico's would prove to be prophetic.

what they believe themselves to be. To be convincing, you do not need honesty or well-thought-out arguments; you need self-belief. George had always been utterly convincing in this sense, whilst David Finlayson had immediately betrayed an incongruity that felt like sleaziness, which was there to some extent. Being a politician he had to lie, and perhaps finding that lying to be degrading, part of him revolted against his professional necessities. In other words, what was good in him was his undoing. He lacked his friend's total self-belief.

By the time he dropped me at the hotel, he was screaming his bile, his rage, his red-hot anger. Some people expect a lot of life, and one of the things they most expect is for people to agree with them always.

One evening at the hotel, I met a German who I initially took to be a journalist. He was tall, slightly uncoordinated in his movements – the sign of someone who moves too little and thinks too much – and severe in his pronouncements. But loquacious too – unusually for a German. Just as I had failed to understand his true profession, that of a staffer at Die Linke, the party to the left of the social democrats in Germany, I failed to realise that he had something important to add to our perception of the referendum until he had been speaking for a while. Although undoubtedly different from the political workers of government parties – more sincere, I would say – he had that overfamiliarity with politics and political thought of those who work full-time in the sector, which means that everything comes out off pat, and the ensuing lack of passion can mislead.

We discussed the media coverage quite a bit, and it was only when he started to move on from this that I became more interested:

"... The days of all power coming out of a gun are over – at least for the moment and let's hope forever. Today you have to rule by manipulation of the facts, which we call propaganda, or you could rule through transparency and genuine trust in the demos."

"The first of these you consider typical of right-wing parties?" I suggested in the knowledge that he was one of the most left-wing of my interviewees in Scotland.

"Not at all, and I'm not just talking about what they call 'red Tories' here, parties once of the left that have discarded all remnants of socialism and enthusiastically espoused neo-liberalism. States, parties and genuine movements of the left have frequently engaged in propaganda, in fact early Soviet propaganda was quite innovative and must have influenced advertising techniques, and under Stalin and Mao the manipulation all but totally obscured reality – an unstable condition for any state.

"There are three reasons for this. Firstly, if your enemy has a powerful weapon, the instinct is to employ it as well. Secondly, when the left was a minority movement, it had trouble getting its voice heard, so it made use not only of lies but also of educative violence; the latter came with disastrous consequences and only strengthened the repressive states of the nineteenth and twentieth centuries. Thirdly, even when their voice was heard, most of the people had been brought up with different values: they didn't only have to be persuaded, their culture also had to be changed."

"Yes, yes. Remember that I'm Italian and Gramsci was one of ours."[37]

"Indeed, but I was speaking of the past. If I were to identify what for me is the most important innovation in this referendum it would be the enfranchisement of the sixteen

---

[37] It was the communist leader and thinker Antonio Gramsci who first suggested that regimes do not rule solely through violence but also through "cultural hegemony", particularly in Europe, and this idea would have a powerful influence on the development of Italian communism as well as other parties and movements of the left throughout the twentieth century.

and seventeen year olds. People thought that this age group was apathetic, but they were proved wrong: the youngsters showed that nothing instructs people like genuine democracy itself."

"I remember interviewing a teenager who supported Yes, and I asked her if the majority of her schoolmates with a vote were going to vote Yes too. She screwed up her face as if to say, 'If only', and then she said, 'But the smart ones are.'"

"Exactly, the smart ones – initially undecided if they're smart – go off and get the information and think it out as individuals. The length of the campaign also helped Yes, by giving people more time to mature their thoughts. We need to learn to trust individuals, because if they think deeply as individuals rather than being dragged along by collective prejudice, then their collective decisions are likely to be more intelligent.

"We look back to and rightly condemn the Narodniks with their exemplary violence, but we forget the Chartists in England. They understood the importance of constitutional change and how it can free people to think. The one reform of theirs that has never been enacted is the annual parliament. Think how that would keep everyone on their political toes. The electorate would be more informed and the representatives more responsive.

"Most people get involved in politics only when they believe that this involvement of theirs can have some influence, however small. And this is entirely rational. They don't turn away from politics out of ignorance or stupidity as the elitist parties of the United Kingdom believe, but because of an entirely rational understanding of their own impotence. Once they reach that state, it's very difficult to draw them back in, but this is what the referendum has done. Some leading politicians have referred to this phenomenon as 'scary'."

"Of course, it would scare them. It challenges their role of necessary mediators."

"Exactly, but they genuinely believe that they're essential

to democracy, and justify all their actions on that basis."

"In your opinion, is the division in this referendum between England and Scotland, or between the Scottish people and the British elite – the establishment, as they call it?"

"Difficult to say. I think that it's more the latter, but there definitely is some of the former. England and Scotland have inevitably converged over the three hundred years of the Union. The same political communities exist in each country, but since the eighties the proportions have been diverging dramatically, ultimately creating a very different overall political culture.

"Germany has different cultural communities too, and their proportions have changed dramatically since the war. I don't say that they are no more Nazis in Germany or they're all in the former DDR, as some in the West claim. Of course there are, and always have been, but they're marginal. Germany really has changed. It didn't happen immediately after the war, but gradually and gained momentum in the sixties and seventies, when we started to process the enormity of what we had done as a nation. People say that self-hate is a bad thing. Maybe it is in some extreme form, but what they mean is self-criticism or even self-awareness. Don't bite the hand that feeds you, they say, but why not if that hand stole or even killed to get the food?

"I approve of my German generation, because on the whole it doesn't love its nation. We're more international, and we rebuild the nation by rejecting the nation as it used to be."

"And what are you building?"

"Ha! It's impossible to say, and it doesn't depend just on us. The British and perhaps even the Italians cannot understand how the histories of France and Germany are so deeply intertwined. Voltaire and the French Enlightenment pointed to the Revolution, but the Revolution wasn't inevitable. The fragmented, powerless, shambolic and ingenuous

Germany described by Voltaire in *Candide* was given a sense of nationhood by Napoleon ..."

"As was Italy ..."

"Indeed, and that German nation was liberal, in the meaning that was used at the time. But it took someone with a very different mindset to unify the country politically, and Bismarck changed us. A demos tired of being pushed around and now undergoing accelerated industrialisation allowed its culture and thinking to be moulded by the settler state of Prussia. Those two Germanies still exist, but the socially liberal social-democratic one is stronger, and in the DDR, where the racist right is getting strong, you'll find socialism still lurking there. Is it the future or a mere ember of the past? The prognosis is not good for a socialist like me, but I'm not going to give up."

I briefly told him about most of my interviews, some I omitted then and some I have omitted here in this book, which is not a day-to-day account of the referendum or a summary of the arguments, but rather an account of how people reacted to it and the ideas it generated. I pointed out that though I agreed that the teenagers were an important element, it was the other end of life the referendum took me to. It was something much more universal, but for me it was original – which says a great deal about my generation. It made me realise that we're not here to consume; we're here to live and then to die. He pulled a face. Not in any religious sense, I hastened to add, or at least not in an afterworld sense, but in the sense that there's nothing beyond the quality of our relationships. This starts with the public thing, with politics, which will never usher in utopia and can only allow us to relate to each other in a manner more inducive to psychological good health.

"I don't want to seduce you into buying or selling, or into voting for this or that. I stand outside such things, though I do secretly or perhaps no longer so secretly wish Yes to win on Thursday. Most of all I want to hear what you and other people have to say, and maybe I'll occasionally respond from my less worked-out mindset, less tidy and sorted out."

"You've learned a lot," he said.

"I have, you know."

"And you're a sadder and a wiser man," he smiled.

I shook his hand and said goodbye. Enough had been said.

XII

The Decision Is Made and What I
Have to Say about All This

When I was a child and witnessed my parents' unnecessarily precarious lifestyle, I always wanted to be rich and secure. Not only did I want that, I also thought that it was a most reasonable desire, as inherent to humans as the desire for food, sleep and sex. Even an urbane man like myself can be surprisingly unaware of the obvious falsehood of his most favoured beliefs. I have learned many lessons during the months I observed the Scottish referendum and since then, but none so important as the fragility and artificiality of the societies we live in. Not that fragility and artificiality are necessarily bad things, but it's inexcusable that I could not perceive them until now.

To some extent, I've come to perceive the Scottish referendum as an epistemological experience: what do we know, what can we know and how can we have a democracy when there is so little reliable information and so much propaganda? Such thoughts are inimical to the journalist's profession, and I had to either suppress them or leave journalism. I arrived at a tacit agreement with the editor that after the referendum I would be moving on. They were keen to lay off staff. So after my altercation with the good professor, I stayed on to witness a historic event.

Scottish independence would only vaguely register with us Italians , and then it would be forgotten in the endless stream of news. The vote finally came after two weeks of intense excitement. The most memorable event for me was the spontaneous festival of hope along Sauchiehall Street, down Buchanan Street and into George Square which took place in Glasgow the Saturday before Referendum Day. It felt as though it was attended by voices that had not been heard but soon hoped to be. Many, like myself, were there by chance and followed the chain of stalls, singers and street artists. It was more of a party than a political rally. The campaign was all but over, and the omens were good.

We shall never know whether or not victory was stolen by a false promise of home rule and devo-max, synonyms for all powers except defence, diplomacy and macroeconomics made verbally by a triad of Unionist leaders, and the delivery of a written document under the authority of that same triad which had no competency – the so-called vow pledging the constitutionalisation of the Scottish Parliament along with five other items also not delivered and too banal to mention. Of course, the first item in the vow could not be granted, because, as almost anyone anywhere interested in politics knows, Britain is a strange and perhaps unique country in that it has no constitution, which must have been known to its authors.

The day after the vote, the streets of Glasgow – a Yes stronghold – were under a dark cloud. The No voters were not celebrating, publically at least, and a few hundred Yes voters gathered to commiserate in George Square, where they were victims of a coordinated attack. There was a sense of shock and disappointment, which was vociferous on the Web, but elsewhere subdued and suffered with a remarkable, silent tenacity.

It came to me not as a bolt of lightning that enlightens and sharpens our focus on life, but as a mist billowing irregularly and inescapably in from the sea, obscuring and confusing as it goes. It changed me, but changed me slowly. The hope it brought was the feeble, bitter-tasting hope of resignation. The hope of someone who has at last learnt to live with their hopelessness. The knowledge it brought was the knowledge of my own ignorance, and with it, the marvellous sense of my own insignificance – and, what's more, the insignificance of each moment in my life compared to my life as a whole: a Russian doll of insignificances.

Would I have changed if I hadn't reported on the Scottish referendum? Or was it merely a moment of reckoning maturing in a discontented man who had never really taken control of his life? Was it just a "midlife crisis"[38] as they call it in English? Invent a name and you invent a reality. After all, was anyone killed? In a world stuffed with injustices sweeping people across the globe as though they were cattle or trapping them in dull, dumb oppression for decades, the Scottish referendum could be seen as a non-event. But wasn't that its secret persuasion? The low-key, mannerly debate, the lack of enormous crowds, the rebirth of school-hall debates – the *comizi* I barely remember from my childhood, only ours were usually held outside in the small squares of small towns, but like these with three or four politicians, activists or journalists speaking and then members of the public joining in.[39] Scotland also had this even lower level of the family debate, often dividing but rarely with viciousness. This was the glimpse of something better: a small nation thinking and genuinely engaging with complex political issues rather than being swept along on a wave of demagoguery, crass headlines, lies and jingoistic manipulation, though these too were certainly there and perhaps won the day. The Scots are not saints, but something about this campaign brought out the best that exists in every nation – not the hysterical crowd fastened by the atavistic instinct of the pack, but a community of thinking

---

[38] "midlife crisis": in English in the original [editor's note].

[39] *comizi*: as suggested, these were generally open-air public meetings for electoral purposes, but the word "rally" implies something bigger.

individuals. It was democracy at last – not acclamation, and no single individual was leading.

Was it nationalism or was it something else? Clearly the independence movement was nationalism in that it wanted the political boundaries to follow a well-established cultural and historical reality. Strangely Scotland as a cultural entity is now primarily political, as its languages are on the brink of extinction, though not irretrievably lost, and it, like Britain as a whole, is in danger of being submerged in a global culture dominated by America. But the referendum was about something more than nation, and independence was supported by people who understood that a nation flows in our blood, but barely touches our senses. A nation is an abstraction, and is never so abstract as when it is our own. And a nation is never so dangerous as when its citizens all agree on what it is, which was not a problem Scotland ever appeared to have.

To what extent was the chance meeting with Maryanne the stimulus that set me thinking? If I remember correctly, I had started to question things before I met her. The stimulus could have been in the inverse direction. I fell in love with her because I had changed or was changing. It may be that we only fall in love fully once in a lifetime. This doesn't mean that we don't have other loves: the closeness of sexual love accompanied by companionship, affairs spiced by the danger of discovery and the overpowering teenage crush that appeared to have enough energy to see it through several lifetimes, yet twenty years later is barely capable of generating a foolish, indulgent smile of incomprehension. These other loves can be even more important, but they are not the discovery of a new land – they are not epiphanic to the same degree. They lack that purity of emotion, because they are in fact hybrids and therefore more capable of surviving in our messy world.

There is some similarity between my attitude to Maryanne

and my attitude to her nation. I wonder if this Scotland of which I have written really exists. I haven't lied, and you'll agree that I have on occasion been brutally and unflatteringly honest about myself and my narcissism. I met those people and had those experiences, but how much do they reflect the country I was trying to explore? – products, as they were, of mere happenchance and wonderment, and my need to interpret their strangeness *to me*. Even the fraudulently virtuous professor, depicted here as something alien and outside Scottish society, must in reality be an integral part of it. Every country is a mix of conflicting forces, and the stranger reads them according to his own beliefs or, quite often, to his desire to jettison his own beliefs in search of new ones. In other words, he experiences something because he wants to experience something. His unconscious has already realised that the way he lives is rotten to its core. He is open to loving a new reality simply because it is different, it is strange. This has been my case; I was ready for change – primed for change – but this does not mean that my interpretation is wrong any more than that it is right. I would argue that it's precisely in these moments of flux that we get closest to understanding this world – or perhaps only to the sensation of understanding this world.

It's not as though I had landed on a South Sea island. What I found in Scotland was not the Noble Savage, not pristine humanity all innocence and creative potential, but mankind who had gone through the *meat-grinder*[40] of history, battered by invasion and marginalisation, by feudal powers and religious fanaticism, by industrialisation and deindustrialisation, and by the elements. This was not a putative Garden of Eden, but the wettest and most windswept part of a wet and windswept isle. The natural and architectural beauties of Scotland are melancholic as much

---

[40] In English in the original [editor's note].

as they are inspiring, and they are often foreboding but rarely hopeful. The uglinesses of Scotland consist in the main of the detritus of consumerism and of the spent force of an industrial era brutally closed off.

I often thought of my Scottish lover. I remembered her body and ached to hold its smoothness in my arms and sense her living, feeling presence. Yet I was firmly resigned to the finality of her rejection of me. I had no desire to pursue her. She was right in her criticism, and firmness of principle was simply part of her character. She was not unforgiving; she simply had no time to waste on the undeserving. I admire this now. It seems wholly rational. I believe her to be a woman destined to a passionate solitude, which is ultimately what she is seeking.

I learned from her rejection that I was not free. I was seduced by wealth but above all by a human intelligence behind that wealth. I was little more than a rat in a cage, conditioned by money that like peanuts was released in measured amounts in return for preset behavioural patterns. Occasionally the hidden intelligence would change the buttons I would need to press and I would quickly readapt.

It was adaptability useful not to me, but to the hidden hand, the intelligence that was both human and systemic. Powerful people made decisions, but they too were governed by the logic of the system currently in vogue, which itself was affected by overproduction, lack of resources, technology, war and natural disasters. We shouldn't mind being a small cog in a system that has some moral purpose, but do we want to be a cog in a system that puts humans and now the planet in peril, and puts as yet unborn generations at risk? Is this not enough to motivate us? Even though our individual powers are miniscule, we can opt out and take the consequences, we can be free, because freedom is nothing more than the ability to think freely, even though external forces are also at play. Freedom is the right to think not what everyone else is thinking. So few of us do this. So few of us realise that we can, but in brief historical periods many of us can and do. Then power reasserts itself. Perhaps inevitably.

Nomen omen. Perhaps I was cursed by the name my eccentric parents gave me, and I have often confessed my rank cynicism to the reader. Now I am more of a sceptic. Philosophically the difference between cynicism and scepticism is paper thin, but in practice – as a means to interpret the world in their current usage – they are poles apart. Both declare that we can never know, but the first says, "Why try?" and the second says, "We must try, however fruitless the results!" And if the cynic comes back with a sarcastic "Is that the best you can do?", the sceptic should say, "Indeed, it is an act of faith in what matters."

"Sounds like a rediscovery of God through the back door."

"Why not," the sceptic voice ends the conversation, "if you want to put it that way? But a different God: less omnipotent, less omniscient and more concerned about His fragile creation!"

And yet I should not be too assertive in my conversion; I should hold on to a little of my cynicism even as I reject it. Each generation has its truth, which in my one was cynicism, and the reason why each generation fails is that it pursues its own truth to the exclusion of all others. That is the route of fanaticism, though it doesn't feel like fanaticism when the great majority accept it as the only truth.

Can cynicism be fanatic? The fanatic always knows, but we find unexpectedly that the cynic and the fanatic are also in some ways similar: they take a truth and turn it into an absolute – and the first produces an absolute negative and the second an absolute positive. No truth can survive such a lack of nuance.

In English they say that there are plenty more fish in the sea, as a balm for the lovesick and rejected. As one who had until then done the rejecting and not the being rejected, I'd had no experience of such sentiments. I'm no longer in search of women to bolster an increasingly fragile self-image. My desire is singular rather than plural, and my desire is contained rather than all-embracing and unquenchable. I must have caught the cold in Scotland. I'm not tired of life, but tired of my life as I have lived it up till now.

I'll travel to where the action is, taking with me this human and political sensitivity. I will live for the day and speak without fear of the consequences. I'll not restrict my experience in order to gain material wealth and comfort. I'll have absolutely no influence at all, but this does not matter. I'm not so foolish as to think that I can change the world. I do this for myself – for a concept I would quite recently have considered laughable: my own integrity.

Having been paid good money not to understand what was going on around me, I have decided to set off with my redundancy money to understand a new situation with no reliable source of income. Perhaps I will start to live for the first time, or that is what the dying man would have said: non-living is a greater danger than death. Or put another way, our fear of insecurity kills our inner life.

Is Europe a nation? Of course it is, and strictly speaking it's not a continent. It has been a nation ever since the Roman Empire and Christianity united it with its varying borders. But today it's a nation in a very real sense: we are different but no longer exotic to each other. I'll go to Greece, which has been tricked and undermined by the Europe in which it believes – whose name it coined. For a while, the heart of Europe's debate was in Scotland in the continent's north-west, now – after a sad defeat – it has moved to the south-east. That'll be my home from now on: the flashpoints of our European nation, and I go not as a revolutionary but as a partial observer.

The Epilogue

or

Manuscript Dispute

(these letters, all written in English, have not been edited except for the punctuation, and are published with their writers' permission just as they arrived at the publisher's office)

Flora MacNeil Cameron
93 Rubh an Eadar-Theangair
Point
Isle of Lewis
HS2 5XU

Robert Rimescioni
Vagabond Voices
Sale Close
Saltmarket
Glasgow

Dear Sir,

It never was the case that a publisher could just take the work of a good man and let another take all the credit, but seemingly this is what a man like you is preparing to do with my husband's work. I saw him working away late into the night on the novel called Chinico, but which you choose to call Travels with a Good Professor, whatever that may mean.

Chinico is seemingly an Italian name, and that's what he called the book. We have a big family and so I could not be always knowing what this book of his was about. I say we but my husband passed away two months ago, but when he was alive I would say to him, "What are you writing, Allan?" and he would reply on those occasions that he did reply, "Chinico, Flora. Chinico, I've told you plenty of times." And I would say, "What language is that?" "Italian," he would reply. "And what does it mean?" "It's a name, just a name. I told you that too, Flora." And off he would go. He was a busy man, always doing something, but God knows what.

I've got a feeling that there's money in this, if you're actually going to publish it as a book. It would be good if all that time he was actually wanting to make us rich.

Yours sincerely,
[signature]

Robert Rimescioni
Vagabond Voices
Sale Close
Saltmarket
Glasgow

Flora MacNeil Cameron
93 Rubh an Eadar-Theangair
Point
Isle of Lewis
HS2 5XU

Dear Mrs Cameron,

I was devastated to hear of you husband's sudden death. You are correct that he was working on a book called *Travels with a Good Professor*, but he was doing so in the capacity of translator and not author. We worked very well together, and I was a great admirer of your husband's work. I certainly don't want to upset you at a time like this, and it's true that I have never talked to or exchanged letters with a man called Cinico de Oblivii, which is an odd surname in Italian and clearly of Latin origin. It's also true that Italy is well known for the variety of its surnames.

I have to tell you that in my conversations with your late husband, he always referred to himself as the translator and he spoke of Cinico as a real person, so unless he was involved in an elaborate hoax, we have to assume that there is a Mr De Oblivii living somewhere and according to the book itself, that somewhere is Greece. I also have to tell you that your late husband always presented the project as one that came with the translation already paid, as according to him Mr De Oblivii paid him for this work out of his own pocket.

However, your news does bring several complications with it, because your husband never presented me with the paperwork. I did mention it several times, but he never quite got round to doing it. I therefore need to get in touch with the author and agree on the contract before publishing the book. If I fail to do this, the book almost certainly will not be published.

Once again my sincere condolences for your husband's untimely death.

Yours sincerely,
[signature]

Flora MacNeil Cameron
93 Rubh an Eadar-Theangair
Isle of Lewis
HS2 5XU

Robert Rimescioni
Vagabond Voices
Sale Close
Saltmarket
Glasgow

Dear Mr Rimescioni,

You yourself say that you have no proof of the existence of this Mr De Oblivii, so how can you insist that he wrote the book. I know my husband, and he often liked to play games and say things that weren't true, not to lie but just to see what might happen.

I spoke to my uncle who knows a lot about these things, and he says that I will have inherited the rights to my husband's book. We should therefore sign a contract. I am willing to do this.

Yours sincerely,
[signature]

Elena Costumanza
via de' Frivoli, 98
50451 Roma
Italy

Robert Rimescioni
Vagabond Voices
Sale Close
Saltmarket
Glasgow

Dear Sir,

Why did you reattach the phone on me? I have rights
to some answers. You desire to publish my husband's journal without any acknowledgement of his hard work. You
say that you are publishing it under the name of Allan
Cameron, who is not the author, just the translator.

Let me tell you that my husband, Cinico de Oblivii, was
a very fine man until he went to Scotland at the time of
the referendum. Before that he was a man of this world,
a civilised man who liked to enjoy himself. There's nothing wrong with that. Then he lost interest in money, which
is strange because I always heard that they're very mean
up there – just like the Genovese. He said that he wasn't
coming back to Italy, which is his native country, and he
has gone to live in Greece.

I couldn't understand a word he was saying. His father
was mad of course, so it may be hereditary. I asked him what
was wrong with Italy. Most foreigners really envy us, so it
can't be that bad. He said that it stank of Berlusconi, and
the damage could no longer be undone. These were very
strange things to say – and coming from a man who believed
in nothing, a healthy man physically and psychologically.

You're wrong to imply that we were separated. He lived
in London because of his work, and I would occasionally
visit him. I like going to the Body Shop, and the selection is

173

so much better in England. I like England, you understand, and Scotland of course, which is the same thing. I hadn't even heard of it until all this happened.

Yours sincerely,
[signature]

Robert Rimescioni
Vagabond Voices
Sale Close
Saltmarket
Glasgow

Flora MacNeil Cameron
93 Rubh an Eadar-Theangair
Point
Isle of Lewis
HS2 5XU

Dear Mrs Cameron,

I'm sorry to bring you bad news during your bereavement, but I have finally been able to locate Mr De Oblivii through his wife. It appears that he is now resident in Greece, and I'm afraid that it's certain that he is the author of this work and your husband the translator.

However, the news is not as bad as it may seem. Mr De Oblivii is a singular gentleman and is not at all interested in demanding his rights as the author. The problem lies more with his wife, who strangely seems more interested in defending her husband's rights than he is.

I propose to write to his wife with a view to finding a possible solution which could, at least in part, meet your aspirations.

Yours sincerely,
[signature]

Robert Rimescioni
Vagabond Voices
Sale Close
416 Saltmarket
Glasgow

Elena Costumanza
via de' Frivoli, 98
50451 Roma
Italy

Dear Mrs Costumanza,

Firstly I would like to apologise for the fact that we got cut off on the phone. The situation took an unpleasant turn before you rang me, because it emerged that the translator had died suddenly and quite tragically. The police report claimed that alcohol had contributed to the tragedy, and some locals spoke of an empty whisky bottle close to the body. His widow, however, vehemently blamed depression caused by our meddling with his translation, which she believes to be an original work of fiction. You can understand that in such circumstances, I must proceed with the utmost caution.

I have spoken to your husband and corresponded with Mr Cameron's widow. Clearly the rights belong entirely to your husband, but as I say, the situation is delicate and I don't want to upset the widow if I can avoid it. She has been left with a family of eight children.

Would it be possible to find a solution that satisfies all parties? And I would also like to know if you have in fact read the manuscript in question.

Yours sincerely,
[signature]

Elena Costumanza
via de' Frivoli, 98
50451 Roma
Italy

Robert Rimescioni
Vagabond Voices
Sale Close
Saltmarket
Glasgow

Dear Mr Rimescioni,

My condolences to the translator's widow. I hope that my husband's odious writings didn't drive hers to this end.

Yes, I have read the original Italian version of this so-called book, and I have completely "changed my tune". This is a profoundly dishonest work, which is not suited for publication.

I do not speak only of its unjust portrayal of myself, but above all of the mendacity and narcissism Cinico claims to have put behind him. He says that he is autocritical, but he isn't really. When he claims to be converted to some kind of truth, isn't he just as hypocritical as the "Good Professor" he derides. What upsets me most is the way my estranged husband presents himself as the stereotypical Italian, which will only confirm foreign prejudice.

I went to Greece to plead with Cinico for our marriage. He lives in a part of Athens where all the anarchists "hang out". I went to see him there. I wanted to reason with him, but when I arrived, I knew it was impossible. It was like hippies without cowbells and lefties without slogans. As far as I could see, they just sat around talking.

He has a relationship with this woman, who was a terrible mess. *Una stracciona.* In rags. She wasn't even young. He must have lost his *senno*, his reason. He said that he wasn't interested in the book any more. If Cameron's widow wants the money, let him have it, he said. It won't be much, he believed. But there is a principle.

When I saw her, I felt disgust not at her, but at my husband. She was filthy – *sudicia*, there's no other word for it. She looked as though she had been dragged across a muddy field by a tractor, though I doubt that she ever left that hellish district of anarchists and "low-lifes" – and certainly never far enough to smell the fresh country air. When I saw her, I realised that Cinico and I could never patch up our dreadful marriage for the sake of our daughter. How could I ever sleep with a man who had slept with that dirty "hag"?

In a way, I felt sorry for her. He'll get her pregnant, if she's not too old for it. He always was careless in that sense. I remember the girl in Portofino and the other one in Manchester, but at least I didn't have to sort that last one out. And those are just the ones I know about.

He'll get her pregnant, and a couple of years later he'll "pike off" to Spain or wherever the new action is. He thinks that he has changed, but he works just as he did before, but in a different circle and for less money. The cretin!

Men like Cinico are forever little boys – just playing at things. Never taking responsibility for others. No loyalty. No real kindness. Just egotism.

So he's angry at the way the world is run, and that's understandable. Who believes that our politicians are honest, let alone wise? But only a child thinks that they can do something about it. Does he seriously think that he can change the world? Then he's more deluded than I thought he was. If he felt so strongly, he could have spent a little less on drink and women, and little more on charity. Instead he abandoned his child, and is unlikely to stand by any other one he has.

I asked for a printout of his manuscript and he wasn't very desirous of that. But he did, because I would not leave him in peace. I didn't start reading it until I was on the plane back to Italy.

The book you want to publish is imbecilic, do you understand? This Scottish Marianne is obviously a complete invention. "A flight of fancy." Does he think that he's the Scottish Delacroix with a pen in place of a paintbrush? He isn't capable of a relationship like that – he isn't capable of loving anyone in any way, not as father and not as a husband. I doubt that this woman existed any more than the French painter's *barricadiera*. This is not a journal, this is fiction "pure and simple". Do your really believe that this collection of fantasies and distortions can throw light on your referendum?

You may like to know that my husband met your translator in the Criterion Bar in Stornoway during his tour of Scotland – not exactly a "literary salon" of the most high order. He told me in Athens that they had a long and interesting conversation, but Cameron was drunk for almost the entire evening. My husband told me that he had never heard Italian spoken with such a drunken "accent". Not, I assume, the kind of company a "bona fide" publisher would want to keep.

I wash my hands of the whole affair. If you are foolish enough to publish this book, you will make yourself a "laughing stock".

Yours sincerely
[signature]

Cinico de Oblivii
46 Peripatet Walk
Athens
Greece

Robert Rimescioni
Vagabond Voices
Sale Close
Saltmarket
Glasgow

Dear Robert,

I want to put down on paper some clarifications about my book, *Travels with a Good Professor*. My wife is correct to say that my self-criticism is less than fulsome, but confessions were not the purpose of my journal. Perhaps my encounter with a radical Yes campaigner could have been excluded, and could be considered extraneous to the campaign itself. On the other hand, I decided that I should write a disquisition on the periphery of this debate, as the main arguments for and against had already been written by autochthonous authors in a manner much better than I could ever achieve.

I can assure you that the woman I've called Maryanne really exists, though this was not in fact her name and very probably I was referencing the French archetype when I chose to call her that. But then every story ever told has grains of untruths and concealments in it. This is not some post-modernist cliché, but rather the assertion that telling the truth is the aim to do precisely that, whether or not the reader is convinced or likely to be convinced. The most mendacious texts are the ones that aim solely at verisimilitude – the truest deceit.

Who cares about the name on a work? If a work has something to say, then publish it, read it, criticise it or throw it to the other end of the room. Now I'm a witness to what's happening in Greece – an unhappier affair. My pen is untiring because the times require it. I listen and record. I observe and reflect but I have no fancy way with words – in any language. I write not out of any *estro letterario*, literary inspiration, I suppose you would say in English, but "inspiration" is a much flatter word and matches *ispirazione*. I write for a purpose.

I may never return to my native land, but I shall always carry its language in my head, and wouldn't want to write in any tongue that wasn't my own dutiful and expressive one. So I will write this second book on Greece in Italian and if it has the same lack of success in Italy as the present one, then I will send the manuscript to you for your consideration.

It is the Europe of peoples – so many peoples constantly mixing and holding apart – that attracts me, that I believe in almost as an act of faith, and not the Europe of banks and neo-liberal hankerings and fantasies. It is the Europe of many languages and the Europe of religions: Catholic, Atheist, Protestant, Agnostic, Orthodox, Muslim and the hybrids such as Uniate and Anglican. It is the Europe of all the great political movements and credos. It is, above all, the Europe of class, and currently the destruction of all the gains the working class made after the Second World War should concern us most. These are being stripped away and must be regained. And in this the European Union is both the solution and the obstacle. It is the Europe that could go in two directions: towards a more equal and generous Europe or towards a more unequal Europe where people satisfy their hunger on a poisonous diet of xenophobia and other forms of hatred. Who would want to remain silent in such times, even if one's voice is barely heard? It is the act itself that liberates us and calms our consciences.

Best wishes,
[signature]

Acknowledgements

This novel could not have been completed without the support of others: my thanks to Sarah MacKelvie for the loan of her house on Eriskay in June 2016, to Roberto, Luisa, Giovanni, Laura and Alessandro Polidori for their fantastic hospitality and Dante Polidori for the use of his splendid flat in Pitigliano in October 2016, and to Faber Residència in Olot, Catalonia in February 2017 for the most comfortable and companionable sojourn I could imagine. These gave me the time and distance to write, and I hope that this book is worthy of their generosity.

I am also indebted to many people for their stories sometimes told to me many decades ago. The story of the "representative Englishman" is the fusion of a fellow van driver's account of his life at a company I worked for in the early seventies and my mother's cousin Morag MacDonald's experience of working in Austria during in the late thirties. Where possible I have relied on actual events in my portrayal of our European nation, but occasionally I have exerted the novelist's prerogative, as in the case of the Estonian, whose physiognomy was suggested by a Dutchman drinking his beer at a bar in Amsterdam airport. Only very occasionally is the dialogue suggested by real events, one of these was the encounter with the Ukrainian. Perhaps it was the only one.

The principal characters are wholly my inventions, and yet in part they inhabit the world I was privileged to enter because I published Jim Sillars' referendum book, *In Place of Fear II*. I refer very little to the cogent arguments of the public debate, but that debate is the essential backdrop to this work, and so my thanks to Jim and the many other panellists who spoke with him.

As always I have relied upon the support of colleagues such as Dana Keller, Mark Mechan and Craig Brown and my thanks to them.